SLAUGHTER AT REBEL RIDGE

SLAUGHTER AT REBEL RIDGE

ROBERT VAUGHAN

WOLFPACK
PUBLISHING
— EST 2013 —

Slaughter at Rebel Ridge
Paperback Edition
Copyright © 2024 Robert Vaughan

Wolfpack Publishing
701 S. Howard Ave. 106-324
Tampa, Florida 33609

wolfpackpublishing.com

Paperback ISBN 978-1-63977-164-6
eBook ISBN 978-1-63977-163-9
LCCN 2024930912

SLAUGHTER AT REBEL RIDGE

ONE

THE LITTLE TOWN WAS HOT, DRY, AND DUSTY. IT had grown up in the middle of nowhere and now sat baking in the sun like a lizard. To the three riders approaching from the west, the collection of adobe and sun-bleached wooden buildings were so much a part of the land it looked almost as if the town were the result of some natural phenomenon, rather than the work of man.

Out on the edge of the town, its civic-minded citizens had erected a sign which read:

COPPERFIELD

POPULATION 412

FRIENDLY, INDUSTRIOUS, PROGRESSIVE

COME GROW WITH US

Olie Minner, the youngest of the three riders, slipped his canteen off the pommel and took a sip. The water was tepid, but his tongue was dry and swollen. He wiped the back of his hand across his mouth, then recorked the canteen and hung it back on his saddle.

"Don't you think, maybe, we could stop at a saloon and get us a few beers afore we take care of our business?" he asked. "It's goin' to take a beer to wet this dryness."

"You just had a drink of water," Leo McCoury answered.

"Yeah, but this water's beginnin' to taste like piss."

"We ain't goin' into no saloons in this town," Leo said. Leo McCoury was the leader of the three. He was also the oldest, though he was only twenty-one.

"If we start drinkin' with the locals, then the next thing you know, ever'one's goin' to have a good description of us."

"Hell, Leo," Bert Thatcher said. "You think they ain't goin' to have a good description of us anyway, the moment we rob that bank of theirs?" He hawked up a spit. "Lookee there," he added. "I ain't got enough wet to even spit proper."

"They ain't goin' to recognize us if we do this job right," Leo ordered. "If you do just like I tell you, we'll be into that bank, have the money, and then be out of here again afore anyone in this town knows what hit 'em." He smiled at the other two. "Then when we ride into the next town, we can go in in style. We'll have enough to swim in beer if we want to. Women, hotels, restaurants, some gamblin' money...hell, we can do anything we want."

"You ever know'd anyone to get 'im two whores at the same time?" Olie asked.

Bert laughed. "Two whores? Hell, you ain't never had one yet, have you?" he asked.

"Why, sure I have, lots of times," Olie insisted. "Whenever I got the money, that is, which, most of the time, I don't."

"Well, you just do what I tell you to today, and you'll have all the money you need...even enough for two whores at the same time if you think you can handle that," Leo said. "Now, let's get on with it. You two boys, check your pistols."

The three men pulled their pistols and checked the cylinders to see that all the chambers were properly charged. Then they slipped their guns back into their holsters.

"Ready?" Leo asked.

"Ready," Olie replied.

Bert nodded in the affirmative.

The three men rode on into town, then pulled up in front of the small bank. Leo and Bert dismounted and handed their reins to Olie, who remained in the saddle and kept his eyes open on the street out front. Leo and Bert looked up and down the street once, then they pulled their kerchiefs up over the bottom half of their faces and, with their guns drawn, pushed open the door.

There were three customers in the bank when Leo and Bert rushed in. Because of the masks on the robbers' faces and the guns in their hands, the customers and the bank teller knew immediately what was going on.

"You fellas! Get your hands up and stand over against the wall!" Leo shouted to the three customers.

The three customers complied with the orders.

Leo hopped over the railing to go behind the teller cage, then held his sack out toward the teller. "Put all your money into this sack," he growled.

Trembling, the teller emptied his cash drawer.

"They ain't much there," Leo growled. "Get the rest out of the safe."

"I can't open the safe," the teller protested. "I don't know the combination."

"What the hell do you mean you don't know the combination? You work here, don't you?"

"Ye-yes," the teller stuttered. "But Mr. Burleson owns the bank. And he's the only one who knows the combination."

"All right, get him."

"He's out of town for the day," the teller replied. "He won't be back until late this evening."

Suddenly the front door opened and Olie, who didn't have the bottom half of his face masked, stuck his head in.

"Leo, Bert, come on quick," he shouted. "Somebody seen these fellas with their hands up and went runnin' down the street for the sheriff. We got to get out of here!"

"Olie, you stupid sonofabitch!" Bert shouted angrily. "You told 'em our names!"

"Open the damn safe!" Leo shouted, pointing his pistol toward the teller and cocking it.

The teller began to shake uncontrollably. "Mister," he said. "Don't you think I would if I could? I don't want to die for someone else's money. I can't open that safe."

With a shout of frustrated rage, Leo brought his pistol down on the teller's head. With a groan, the teller dropped to the floor. Then, with the sack of money firmly clutched in his hand, Leo vaulted back over the teller's counter.

"Let's go!" he shouted.

As they reached the front door of the bank, someone from across the street fired at them with a heavy-gauge shotgun. The charge of double-aught buckshot missed the three robbers, but it did hit the front window, bringing it down with a loud crash.

Leo shot back and though he missed the man with the shotgun, he at least drove him back inside. The three bank robbers leaped into their saddles then started at a gallop down the street.

There had been several citizens out on the street and the sidewalks when the shooting erupted, and now they stood there watching in openmouthed shock as the three men who had just robbed their bank were getting away. Either none of them were armed, or else none of them wished to be a hero, for other than the one attempt with a shotgun when the three men had first emerged from the bank, no one made any attempt to stop them.

At the end of the street, a man stepped down off the boardwalk and out into the street. A flash of sunlight revealed the fact that a star was fastened to his vest.

"It's the sheriff!" Leo shouted. Leo shot at the sheriff, and the sheriff grabbed his shoulder, then staggered back a step. Leo shot a second time, as did Bert and Olie, and this time the sheriff went down under the fusillade of bullets.

By now the three men were out of town and pushing their horses hard to put as much distance between them and the town as they could.

"Is anyone comin' after us?" Leo shouted.

Olie, who was bringing up the rear, looked over his shoulder at the receding town. He saw no riders.

"No," he answered. "They ain't got no one mounted. We got away clean!" He laughed out loud, whooping into the wind. "We got away clean!"

* * *

DANE CALDER COULD TELL by the way the outlaws were riding that they knew someone was on their trail. They didn't know who it was or how many were after them, but they did know they were being dogged. They hadn't built a fire in the last three days, which meant that they, like Dane, were making do with cold jerky and tepid water.

Eating in the saddle didn't bother Dane. Having spent a while with the Apache, there were times when jerky and water would seem like a feast. He knew it was hard on the men he was trailing though, because he had already found a couple of pieces of barely chewed jerky...spit out, no doubt in anger over having to eat such fare.

The three outlaws who held up the bank in Copperfield had gotten away with less than two hundred dollars because the teller had managed to convince them that the rest of the money was in the vault and he couldn't get to it. The robbery was bad enough, but on the way out of town, they also killed Percy Santos, the deputy sheriff. Actually, the deputy hadn't really represented any particular threat to the three young robbers. Santos was an old man who had been given the job almost as an act of charity. He didn't even carry a gun and served mostly as a cook for the few drunks and the occasional hell-raising cowhands who were the most frequent residents of the jail.

As a result of killing the old man, Leo McCoury, Olie Minner, and Bert Thatcher were now wanted for murder. The town of Copperfield had offered a $250 reward for each of the men and the Arizona territorial government had added another $250. That made the three men worth a total of fifteen hundred dollars... enough money to interest Dane Calder.

Dane was a bounty hunter. He wasn't just any bounty hunter—he was the most feared bounty hunter in the whole territory.

The trail led into a canyon which Dane didn't like very much. There were too many opportunities for the outlaws to set up an ambush. He stopped for a moment and listened hard, trying to hear anything from ahead...the whicker of a horse, a voice, even the scratch of iron-shod hooves on stone. He could hear nothing.

Dane took a deep breath and pulled his rifle from the saddle sheath, then started into the canyon. He hadn't ridden more than a hundred yards into the canyon before all the hackles stood up on the back of his neck. He hadn't heard anything, nor had he seen anything. But in that sixth sense developed by men who constantly live on the verge of instant death, he had felt something. He pulled his horse to a stop just as a bullet fried the air not six inches in front of his face. It hit a big rock on the other side of the trail, then whined off into space while the canyon reverberated with the flat crack and high-pitched scream of the missed rifle shot. If he had not stopped at that very moment, he would have been killed.

With his rifle in his hand, Dane slid down quickly. He slapped his horse to get him out of the line of fire, then ran toward a nearby line of large rocks, diving for cover just as another shot rang out. This one, like the first, was so close that he could hear the bullet passing.

"Who are you?" a voice called from a position partway up the canyon wall. "What are you doggin' us for?"

"The name's Calder," Dane called back. As soon as he shouted, he rolled to his right. This, too, was a fortunate move, for a bullet kicked up sand and pebble at the exact spot where he had been. Whoever was handling the long-gun up there was pretty good.

Dane moved to the end of the row of rocks and studied the canyon wall on the opposite side. There was no way he could get over there to them unseen, because he was on one side of the trail and they were on the other. He would have to cross an open space to start up the canyon wall and when he did that, he would be seen.

"You that bounty hunter ever'body talks about?" Like the rifle shots before, the words echoed back and forth through the canyon.

"That's me," Dane shouted.

Again, he rolled right after he called. This time, though, as he came out of the roll, he had the rifle to his shoulder, looking out across the barrel at the canyon wall toward the sound of the outlaw's voice. He saw the puff of smoke from the outlaw's rifle, then saw the outlaw raise up, slightly, to check on where his bullet had gone. It was a fatal move on the part of the outlaw, because for that one second, Dane had him in his sights. One second was all he needed. He squeezed the trigger, and the Winchester roared and kicked back against his shoulder. A second later, the outlaw tumbled down the wall on the other side of the canyon.

"Leo? Leo, are you hit?" a frightened voice called. "Bert! Bert, I think he got Leo! What are we goin' to do?"

"There's still two of us agin the one of him," Bert answered.

"But he's got us trapped up here!"

"Olie's right, Bert," Dane called. "I do have you trapped up there."

"And we got you trapped down there," Bert replied.

"Uh-uh," Dane said. "I've got my water and food with me. I'll just bet you fellas left yours with your horses."

"He's right, Bert! We ain't got no water or nothin' up here."

"Shut up, Olie," Bert called. "See if you can get a look at where he's at."

"I ain't movin' from here," Olie replied fearfully.

"You yellow sonofabitch," Bert snarled. "I'll take care of him. Then I'll take care of you."

Bert began firing then. He wasn't as accurate as Leo had been, and that gave Dane a chance to improve his own position without fear of being hit. Crouching over, Dane ran behind the line of rocks, then darted across the little open gap so that he was on the same side of the trail as the two outlaws.

"Did you get him?" Olie called. From the sound of Olie's voice, Dane knew that he was no more than twenty yards away. He began looking around for a way up to him.

"I don't know," Bert called. Bert was a little farther into the canyon.

"You must'a got him. I don't see him or hear him movin' around down there."

Dane smiled. He realized then that he had managed to cross the trail unseen.

"Shoot again," Olie called.

"You shoot," Bert replied. "I'll keep an eye open and if he returns your fire, I'll have him."

"The hell with that. I ain't makin' myself no decoy," Olie said.

"Shoot at him, you sonofabitch, or I'll shoot at you," Bert growled.

Dane saw Olie raise up then. Unlike the others, who had rifles, Olie was armed only with a pistol. He began shooting wildly. While Olie was shooting and looking anxiously toward the rocks where Dane had been, Dane managed to climb up a fissure until he was just a few feet away. He waited until the hammer on Olie's gun fell on an empty chamber.

"All right, I shot at him," Olie called. "Now I got to reload, it's your time."

"You dumb bastard, you didn't do nothin' but waste your bullets," Bert replied.

Olie turned around and slid back down to a seated position with his back against the rock, believing that way he was protected from Dane. He took a box of shells out of his shirt pocket, poured some into his hand, then began punching out the spent cartridges so he could push in the new. Dane waited until that moment, then leaped quickly across the gap, landing right in front of Olie.

"What the hell?" Olie shouted in surprise. That was as far as he got before Dane hit him with the butt of his rifle.

"Olie? Olie, what's goin' on over there? What'd you yell for?"

Dane stood up then and looked toward the sound of Bert's voice. It took him a few seconds, but he finally saw Bert squatted down behind a big rock. Like Olie, Bert was protecting himself from someone he thought was on the opposite side of the trail. But, like Olie, he was totally exposed.

"Give it up, Bert," Dane said easily. "I've got a bead on you."

Surprised by the nearness of the challenging voice, Bert looked around, then saw that Dane was right. There was nothing left for him to do but throw down his rifle. With a sigh, he did so.

"What's goin' to happen to us now?" he asked.

"I'm takin' the two of you in."

"To be hung?"

"Probably."

Bert looked over to where Leo had been. "Did you kill Leo?"

"Yes."

Bert sighed. "He's got the best of it, then."

Two

THAT SAME DAY, IN THE SMALL TOWN OF Dudleyville, the normal afternoon's commerce was taking place when a rider came into town. He pulled up near the saloon, dismounted, and tied his horse to the hitchrail. He was rail-thin, with flat, gray eyes and several days' growth of beard. He took off his hat and rubbed a handkerchief across his face, then stuck the handkerchief back into his pocket. He glanced up and down the street as if making certain there was no potential threat, then pushed his way through the swinging batwing doors.

He was wearing a gun strapped low on his right hip, and once inside, he stepped away from the door so he wasn't backlighted, then paused for a moment before he moved on. Only when his eyes were fully adjusted to the dimmer light did he walk over to the bar.

"You know who that is?" one of the saloon's patrons whispered to his table partner.

"Can't say as I do."

"That there is Frank Colby. I reckon you've heard of him, ain't you?"

"Yeah, I've heard of him. He's a…"

"He's a gunfighter," the first one interrupted, as though he didn't want to be cheated out of imparting the information.

"He's supposed to be…"

"Really fast," the first one said.

"What do you reckon he's doin' here?"

"I don't know. Look at that gun handle. You think there's any notches on it?"

"I don't know, and I don't aim to look none too close."

Colby, unaware he was the subject of a whispered conversation—or perhaps aware, but unconcerned—stepped up to the bar and slapped a coin down.

"Whiskey," he grunted.

"I'll be glad to serve you some whiskey, Mr. Colby. Only we ain't got no blended whiskey left. That cowboy down there just bought our last bottle. Our trade liquor ain't that bad though."

Colby turned to look at the cowboy. "I'd like to buy the whiskey from you," he said.

The cowboy shook his head. "Mister, I been eatin' trail dust for two weeks thinkin' about comin' in here for a good bottle of whiskey. I aim to keep it for myself."

"I'll pay double."

"That's mighty generous of you, but thank you, no. I plan to keep it."

Colby put some money on the bar and slid it toward the cowboy.

"Mister, don't you hear good?" the cowboy asked. "I told you, I ain't sellin' my whiskey."

"Either pick up the money or go for your gun," Colby said.

"What?"

"I said, pull your gun or give me the bottle."

"You're aimin' to throw down on me over a bottle of whiskey?"

"Give him the bottle, boy," the bartender said. "Don't you know who this is?"

"I don't know, and I don't care," the cowboy said. "I don't plan to oblige 'im with a gunfight or the bottle."

Colby pulled his gun and fired. Pink mist sprayed from the cowboy's earlobe and he slapped his hand up to the side of his head with a howl of pain. By the time the smoke cleared, the pistol was back in Colby's holster.

"Give me the bottle," Colby ordered.

With his left hand still pressed against his ear, the cowboy shoved the bottle down the bar with his right. "Here," he said. "Take the damn bottle." He reached for the money.

"Leave it," Colby said. "You didn't take it when I offered it to you."

The cowboy stared at Colby through hate-filled eyes, then, still keeping his hand pressed against the side of his head, rushed out of the saloon. Colby poured himself a drink, then turned back to the bar, studying, carefully, the mirror behind the bar.

"He didn't mean nothin' by challengin' you like that, Mr. Colby," the bartender said. "He's just a boy, that's all."

"You know of a town name of Rebel Ridge?" Colby asked as he raised the glass to his lips.

"Sure do. It's 'bout ten, maybe fifteen miles north of here," the bartender said. "It's a mining town. You goin' there?"

Colby tossed the liquor down, then slid the glass across the bar to indicate that he wanted another.

"A friend of mine is the sheriff over there. I hear he is putting on deputies. Thought I might join him."

"You mean you're goin' to be a deputy?" the bartender asked in surprise. "I never would've thought you would be a..." Suddenly the bartender realized that he might be overstepping his bounds, so he swallowed the last of his sentence. "'Course," he added. "I'm sure you would make a fine deputy."

Someone got up from one of the tables then, and walked over to the end of the bar. He had red hair and a red beard, and Colby saw that he had been studying him fairly intently from the moment he had entered the saloon.

"Hey, you, Colby," he finally said.

Colby looked toward him, but he didn't speak.

"That is your name, ain't it? Ain't you Frank Colby?"

"If you're a bounty hunter, mister, there's no paper out on me," Colby said.

"I ain't no bounty hunter."

"You got somethin' stickin' in your craw, mister. What is it?" Colby asked.

"The name is Martin. My brother was Syd Martin. Does that name mean anything to you?"

"Can't say as it does," Colby replied.

"He was a deputy sheriff up in Rodsburg. It still doesn't mean anything to you?"

Colby turned away from the bar so that he was facing Martin.

"I had a little scrape up in Rodsburg once," he said.

"A little scrape, you call it? Mister, I don't call killin' a little scrape," Martin said.

"I guess that all depends on who's gettin' killed," Colby said.

"It was my brother who got killed," Martin said.

"Yeah, well, like I said. It was a little scrape. Better him than me."

"I've chased you to hell and back, you sonofabitch!" Martin shouted.

At the sound of Martin's words of challenge, everyone in the saloon began making haste to move out of the way. Tables scraped against the floor and chairs turned over as the men hurried out of any potential line of fire.

"You found me. What do you aim to do now?"

Martin stepped away from the bar and held his hands out to either side.

"As you can see, I'm not armed," he said. He doubled up his fists. "But I don't need a gun to take the likes of you."

As Martin started toward Colby, Colby pulled his pistol and shot Martin in the right knee. The impact of the bullet knocked Martin down.

"Stay down there, and you might live," Colby said.

Using the bar to assist him, Martin got back onto his feet. The wound in his right knee was bleeding profusely and the bottom of his trouser leg was already soaked with blood.

Colby shot him again, putting a ball in his left knee. When Martin went down this time, he was unable to get up.

"Give me a gun," Martin said to the bartender. His voice was racked with pain.

"Martin, let it go," the bartender said.

"I said give me a gun, dammit!" Martin repeated louder and with more insistence.

"Give him a gun," Colby said quietly.

"You don't want to..."

"Give him a gun," Colby said again. He neither raised his voice nor changed the inflection but said the words as flatly and unemotionally as if he had just inquired of the time.

With a sigh, the bartender pulled a pistol from behind the bar, then leaned over to hand it down to Martin.

"Put the gun on the floor in front of you," Colby ordered.

"I should've shot you in the first place, you bastard," Martin growled as he laid the gun on the floor.

Colby smiled a small, evil smile. "Whenever you feel lucky," he said.

Martin took a deep breath, then made a desperate grab for the gun. Colby watched him and waited until Martin had the gun in his hand and was raising it from the floor before he even began his own draw. Then, as he was still bringing his pistol up, Colby drew and fired. His bullet caught Martin in the chest and pitched him back onto the floor. His arms flopped uselessly beside him and the unfired gun fell into a half-full spittoon.

Colby looked at his victim for a moment, then put the pistol back in his holster. He reached for the bottle of whiskey.

"Can't say as I got a very warm reception here," he said to the bartender. "Think I'll mosey on up to Rebel Ridge, where I've got friends. I figure I'll be a bit more welcome there."

Colby walked through the door, while behind him a cloud of gun smoke drifted slowly toward the ceiling and a man lay dead on the barroom floor. Once outside, without so much as a glance back into the saloon, Colby mounted his horse and rode away. The bottle of blended whiskey glinted once in the sun.

* * *

REBEL RIDGE BEGAN as a mining town. For more than two years, the Consolidated Mining Company had taken as much silver out of the Rebel Ridge digs as had been mined at any other place in the country. Now, though most of the silver veins were played out, there was still a large amount of copper remaining. This allowed the more settled hard-rock miners to make a living, though the work was harder and the payoff less.

During Rebel Ridge's heyday there had been more than one way to mine silver. Some did it with a pick and shovel; others did it with cards, or liquor, or a pretty smile and a well-shaped thigh.

Not everyone was upset with the playout of the silver mines. Silver, like gold, attracted get-rich-quick people. Copper, on the other hand, tended to attract only the most industrious of the miners...the mining engineers and the hardworking men who went down into the shafts. These were the steady, sober-minded men who wanted to start families and build a town. That also tended to attract stores, banks, schools, doctors, and freight and stage lines. There were also a few ranches nearby to take advantage of the railroad. That was what the citizens of Rebel Ridge wanted, and was what was happening, until a man named Jesse Lowman had other ideas.

Jesse Lowman was a short, unattractive man with a pockmarked face, a drooping black beard, a hawk-like nose, and narrow, obsidian eyes. It was, perhaps, that unattractiveness which made him an outcast from society. As a result, he had developed absolutely no social skills. He did, however, have one skill which marked him as a man with whom others would have to reckon. Jesse Lowman was a deadly shot, snake-fast on the draw, and with so few moral compunctions about killing, he could take the life of another as easily as he could step on a cockroach.

Lowman had come to Rebel Ridge when the mines were still producing silver. He had been hired by the mining company to provide security for the silver shipments. Some, who knew of Lowman's spotted past—

he had robbed a few banks and held up a stage or two —suggested using him to guard the silver was like setting the fox to watch the hen coop. Others insisted that you must "set a thief to catch a thief" and saw no problem whatsoever using Lowman to guard the shipments.

After the silver played out, however, there was no longer a need to provide guards over the ore shipments. That was because it took so much copper to turn a profit that the freight wagon gave way to the railroad as the prime carrier. Thus, by the time Consolidated Mining completed its changeover from silver to copper, Lowman and his men found themselves out of work.

Those who breathed a sigh of relief over that fact soon learned, to their dismay, that Lowman had no intention of leaving Rebel Ridge. Instead, he bullied a few of the town's officials into appointing him as the town sheriff, and his men as deputies. Now, with badges on their vests, the Lowman gang had free run of the entire town.

His reign of terror began with the saloon, where he extracted a "tax" from each drink, supposedly to pay for his protection. That quickly extended to the other businesses in town as well—hotels, restaurants, stores, even the livery stable.

In addition to the tax Lowman and his deputies collected, they enjoyed the privilege of a "special reduced rate" for the goods they bought from any of the town's merchants. What they paid was so little that it was practically stealing. Always bullies, they moved along the boardwalks or through the streets of the town, pushing any and all out of their way. They would sometimes go so far as to pistol-whip some poor soul who was too slow to avoid them. There had even been a few killings, usually over a dispute in a card game, but always justified as "self-defense" or "killed while resisting arrest for card cheating."

The situation eventually reached the point where very few of the decent citizens of Rebel Ridge would dare venture out of their homes. That hurt the business of the town's merchants, and as the legitimate stores began closing, the town began dying.

As Rebel Ridge started to die, however, it flared brightly in a different way, for drinking, gambling, and whoring became its major industries. News of the "wide-open" town spread throughout the territory, and it began to attract new residents. The new residents, however, were not the kind of people the original citizens of the town wanted, for they were nothing more than carbon copies of Lowman and his men. As more hoodlums arrived, the number of those who were sucking out the life's blood of the town became disproportionate to the number of those whose industriousness supplied the life's blood of the town. Like an animal being drained by leeches, the town was slowly but inexorably sinking to its knees.

This was the condition of things when Frank Colby arrived in Rebel Ridge. It took him only a few minutes to find Jesse Lowman and offer his services.

"Frank, you old saddle tramp, you," Lowman greeted him warmly. "How long has it been? A year? Two years?"

"Nearly three," Colby said. "Back in Dodge, I think."

"Yeah, Dodge City," Lowman said. He smiled. "It was a wide-open town then. Like Rebel Ridge is now. So you want to be a part of it, do you?"

"If you got room for me," Colby replied.

"Hell, I always got room for a good man," Lowman said. "Outside of Bucky Zorn, I don't have anyone around me who's worth a pitcher of piss."

"Why do you keep 'em around, then?"

"The more deputies I have, the more scared the locals are," Lowman explained. "And the more scared they are, the easier it is to keep things under control."

"Are the pickin's good enough to go around?"

"If you know where to pick," Lowman replied with a smile. "Tell you what. If you want to stay on and help me run things around here, I'll make you my second deputy."

"Your second deputy?"

"Bucky is the first."

"Don't think I've ever heard of this Bucky."

"He's a big sonofabitch," Lowman said. "Half man and half bear. He's good to have around. He can keep more people straight with his fists than I can with a gun...and without havin' to kill anyone."

"It don't bother me to kill anyone," Colby said.

Lowman laughed. "Hell, me neither, when it needs doin'. But we're the law in Rebel Ridge, and we got to think that way. We can't just go round killin' the citizens 'cause we feel like it."

"What do I get as your second deputy?"

"Me, you, and Bucky split the business tax,"

Lowman said. "That's where the real money is. The others have to collect a personal tax. The personal tax is pretty slim pickin's, and it's gettin' slimmer. Now what do you say? Are you in?"

Colby smiled. "Yeah, sure, why not?" he asked. "It might be fun bein' a deputy."

THREE

To the three cowboys approaching Rebel Ridge after dark that evening, there was little sign that the town way dying. The bright glow of lights from the busy saloons was visible from far out in the desert, and as they drew even closer to the town, they could hear the sounds of reverie: loud voices, the high-pitched trill of a woman's laughter, and the tinkling of pianos.

"They's three things I want when I get to town," one of the cowboys said. Though his real name was Edgar Yokum, he was known to everyone as Poke. "I want me a steak, a bottle of whiskey, and a woman."

"You got them three things just backward, Poke," Lanny said. "I aim to get me a woman, a bottle of whiskey, and then a steak."

Eli laughed at the other two. "Why you fellas want to take the time to mess with a steak and a bottle of whiskey beats me," he said.

"You mean you aim to just get a woman?" Poke asked.

"That ain't what I mean a'tall," Eli said. "I want three things, just like you two boys."

"And what would them three things be?" Lanny wanted to know.

"A woman, another woman, and another woman," Eli said, and all three men laughed.

Like moths drawn to a flame, the three cowboys stopped in front of the Silver Strike Saloon. Built during Rebel Ridge's heyday of silver mining, the Silver Strike had a real mahogany bar, a gilt-edged mirror, and an ample supply of a decent grade of whiskey. There were several large jars of pickled eggs and sausages on the bar and a fresh-daily supply of towels tied to rings every few feet on the customers' side of the bar to provide the drinkers with a means of wiping their hands and mustaches. The walls were decorated with game-heads and pictures. The obligatory reclining nude was behind the bar, while on the opposite wall was a mountain scene, a cool, snow-covered pine forest beneath a silver moon and a starry vault of night sky. In the latter picture, a train, with its huge headlight stabbing forward, was crossing a high, wooden trestle. Every window of every car in the train was unrealistically and brightly lit, and every window had a smiling passenger's face.

All of this had been put in place by Curt Newberry, the saloon's owner and bartender, before Lowman and his bunch had taken over the town. The picture had given the saloon a bit of respectability, though the effort seemed a mockery, now that Lowman was in charge of things.

The upstairs area didn't extend all the way to the

front of the building, so the main room of the saloon was big, with exposed rafters just below the high-peaked ceiling. There were at least a dozen tables in the large common room, and they were arranged around a couple of potbellied stoves. The stoves weren't in use now because it was the middle of August. There was, however, a lingering tang of wood smoke near the stoves, evidence of their use during the winter season.

When the three cowboys pushed through the batwing doors, they were met almost immediately by one of the girls who worked at the saloon.

"Hello, boys," she said with a practiced smile. "My name is Suzie. Welcome to the Silver Strike."

"Well, boys, I got me a girl," Poke said, putting his arm around her. "Ain't that right, Suzie?" He looked at the others. "What are you two goin' to do?"

"Oh, I'm not just your girl, honey. I'm everyone's girl. You ask anyone, they'll tell you. Suzie is everyone's girl."

"For sure?" Poke asked. He laughed. "All right, Suzie, if you want to be everyone's girl, that's jake with me. Come on and have a drink with us."

Suzie laughed. "That's just what I'm planning to do."

What Suzie didn't tell the boys, and what they didn't know, was that she had just left one of the other tables a moment earlier after having had a disagreement with one of the men. The person with whom she had had the disagreement was Slim Collins, who also happened to be one of Jesse Lowman's deputies. The disagreement was over whether or not Suzie would go upstairs with Collins. It wasn't over whether or not Suzie was that kind of a girl...she *was* that kind of a girl. It wasn't over money either, for Collins was more than willing to meet Suzie's price. But Suzie felt that, whore or not, she should be able to say who she would take for a customer and who she wouldn't. Collins was a brutal man who enjoyed hitting women, and Suzie wanted no part of that. Now, as Suzie escorted the three young cowboys to an empty table, she was followed by Collins's angry, staring eyes.

Within half an hour the three young cowboys were well on their way to getting drunk from cheap whiskey. Then, after some bragging about his prowess as a dancer, Poke decided to demonstrate. He got up and began dancing around the table. When his spurs got tangled up, he fell flat on his back. Suzie and the other two cowboys laughed heartily, then Lanny got up.

"You call that dancin'? You can't dance worth a damn," he said. "Look at me, Suzie. Let me show you how it's really done."

Lanny threw his hat onto the floor, then began dancing around it. But, like Poke before him, he tripped. Unlike Poke, however, he didn't fall on the floor. Instead, he fell against one of the other tables. That just happened to be the table where Collins was sitting.

"Get away from me, you drunken bastard," Collins growled, shoving him roughly.

Eli, who was the oldest and least drunk of the three cowboys, saw the badge pinned to Collins's shirt. He saw also that Lanny was about to react to being shoved, so he jumped in, quickly, and apologized.

"My friend didn't mean nothin', Deputy," he said. "We been workin' hard all week and are just tryin' to have a good time, that's all."

"Yeah? Well if he winds up on me again, I'll end his fun...permanent."

The bartender came around from behind the bar then to speak to the deputy.

"Don't be so hard on those boys, Collins. They're just workin' cowboys who don't mean no harm," he said. "I've seen 'em in here before."

Collins pointed to the bar. "Newberry, you just get on back behind the bar there, where you belong," he growled. "This here ain't none of your concern."

"I own the saloon," Newberry said. "If it ain't my concern, whose concern is it?"

Collins pointed to his badge. "I'd say this here comes under the headin' of keepin' the peace," he said. "Now, you go on about your business an' I'll go about mine."

Newberry started to say something else, then thought the better of it. He was as much subject to the whims of the sheriff and his deputies as any other merchant in town, and as resentful of it. With a sigh, he returned to the bar as Collins had ordered.

During the altercation, the piano player had stopped playing, and for a moment there was a dead silence as everyone looked on with interest to see what was about to happen.

"Piano player, play," Poke shouted. "How'n hell can I dance if you don't play?"

"Poke," Eli said. "Poke, maybe you've had enough dancin' for one evenin'."

"Like hell I have," Poke replied. "I come to town to have a good time an' that's what I'm goin' to have. I ain't seen nothin' but the backside of cows for more'n a week now, an' I aim to let off a little steam. Play some music."

The piano player looked over at Newberry, who, with a slight nod of his head, indicated that the music could continue. With that, the piano player turned back toward his instrument and put his fingers on the keyboard. A second later, the saloon was once again filled with the raucous melody of "Buffalo Gals."

The music seemed to ease the tension, and the laughter and conversation resumed as easily as if it had never been interrupted in the first place.

With the situation under control, Eli left Suzie and his two friends and, after a few words of conversation with one of the other girls, went upstairs with her.

"Hey, Poke, do you see where Eli's gone?" Lanny asked a few moments later.

"No, where'd he go?" Poke asked.

"He took him a woman upstairs. I'm goin' to get me one too. You just goin' to dance all night, or what?"

"Yeah, but I ain't goin' to dance by myself," Poke answered. "Come on, Suzie, dance with me," he called, waving his arms to invite Suzie to join him.

Laughing at Poke's antics, Suzie stood up.

"I'd be glad to join you, cowboy," she said. She joined him on the floor, hooked her arm through his, and began to dance.

There were three other men at the table with Collins. Like Collins, they were wearing deputy badges. One of them laughed, then pointed at Poke.

"Hell, I know now why you couldn't get ole Suzie upstairs with you, Collins. You didn't dance none with her. Looks to me like that cowboy has got your girl," he suggested.

"Yeah? Well, I'd like to see how long he's plannin' on keepin' her," Collins answered, unamused by the joke. He got up and started toward the bar. Instead of going directly to the bar, however, his circuitous route took him to where Poke and Suzie were dancing. They didn't notice him approaching, and by now they were oblivious to everything around them except the music, each other, and the fun they were having.

As Collins passed by, he stuck his leg out, then pushed Poke down.

"Hey, mister, what the hell you think you're doin'?" Poke asked angrily.

"Cowboy, you're so drunk you can't even stand up," Collins said. "I guess maybe you'd better spend the night in jail. Come on, you're comin' with me."

"Like hell I am," Poke said, reaching awkwardly for his gun.

"Watch 'im, Collins! He's goin' for his gun!" one of the other deputies shouted, though the warning wasn't necessary, for Collins was already starting his own draw.

With Poke lying on the floor and Collins standing, the advantage was all Collins's as the two men drew their pistols. Collins fired from point-blank range, putting a bullet in Poke's heart before Poke could even clear his holster.

In the meantime, Lanny, who had walked over to

the bar to find his own girl, turned back around just in time to see Collins shooting Poke.

"No!" Lanny shouted, pulling his own pistol. He shot Collins, then was himself cut down by Frank Colby, who, sitting at a table in the back of the room with Bucky Zorn, had just joined the fray.

After the explosions of gunfire, an eerie silence fell over the saloon as the other patrons stood there looking at the three dead bodies, dumbstruck by the suddenness of events. A heavy cloud of blue-black smoke from the three discharges began drifting up toward the top of the room. There was a scampering of feet on the upper-floor landing as the men and women who had been engaged in the private rooms now scampered to the head of the stairs for a look down into the common room to see what had happened.

One of those on the upper landing was Eli Underhill. When he peered over the railing, he saw his two friends lying in pools of their own blood. "Poke! Lanny!" he shouted, starting down the stairs toward them.

"That there's the other one!" one of the deputies who had been sitting at the table with Collins said.

Frank raised his pistol.

"You don't need to shoot," Bucky said, crossing the room in a few quick, long strides. He reached out to grab Eli.

Eli had no idea that he was in danger. As a result he made no effort to get away, which meant that Bucky had no difficulty in apprehending him.

"Hey!" he shouted. "What are you doing? Let me

go! Those are my pals lyin' there. That's Poke and Lanny! Let me go! I've got to see them!"

"Mister, you don't got to do nothin' but go to jail," Bucky growled. Bucky was such a big and powerfully built man he was able to control Eli all by himself.

Four

THERE WAS NO BUILDING SPECIFICALLY DESIGNATED
as a courthouse in Copperfield. As a result of this defi-
ciency, Judge Jeremiah Whitmore, the visiting circuit
judge, had to hold his court in the schoolhouse. That
caused no difficulty, as the school was vacant for the
summer.

Sheriff Aaron Jenson stepped to the front of the
improvised courtroom, then looked out over the
gallery. The place was filled to overflowing with people
who had come to see the trial of the two men Dane
Calder had brought in. Jenson wasn't surprised by the
crowd. Feelings were running high because the deputy
killed by the bank robbers during their escape was one
of the town's most beloved citizens. There was also
some interest in the fact this was a capital trial, the
first ever to be held in Copperfield. Also of notable
intrigue, the fact the desperadoes had been brought in
by none other than the most famous bounty hunter

himself had added a degree of excitement to the situation.

"All rise," Sheriff Jenson said.

There was a scrape of chairs and a rustle of pants, petticoats, and skirts as the spectators in the makeshift courtroom stood. A spittoon rang as one male member of the gallery made a last-second, accurate expectoration of his tobacco quid.

"Oyez, oyez, oyez, this circuit court, meeting in Copperfield, is now in session, the Honorable Judge Jeremiah Whitmore presiding."

Judge Whitmore took his seat in front of the assembly, then looked out over the court through clear, piercing blue eyes.

"Be seated."

The gallery sat, then watched as the two prisoners were brought into the room for the trial.

"Olie Minner and Bert Thatcher, you are charged with bank robbery and murder," Judge Whitmore said. "Are you represented by counsel?"

"They are, Your Honor," a man said, standing to address the court.

"And who are you?"

"I am Foster Smith, Your Honor, duly authorized by the bar to practice law in the Arizona territory."

"And you have been appointed by the court to defend these men?"

"Yes, Your Honor."

"And how do they plead?"

"To the charge of bank robbery, guilty, Your Honor. To the charge of murder, not guilty."

"Very well, let the trial proceed," Judge Whitmore said.

The case for the prosecution was quick and simple. There were three witnesses in the bank during the time of the robbery, all of whom identified the two defendants as having been two of the three men who committed the robbery. There were even more witnesses, nine in fact, who identified them as two of the three men who were involved in the shooting of Deputy Santos. The doctor testified that he took four bullets from the deputy's body, two of which were .44-caliber and two of which were .31-caliber rounds. Leo McCoury was the only one who had been armed with a .44. Both Olie Minner and Bert Thatcher had been carrying .31-caliber pistols.

At the conclusion of the doctor's testimony, Foster Smith stood up for cross-examination.

"Dr. Russell, of the four bullets you took from the deputy's body, can you determine which one killed him?"

"There were two which would have been fatal," the doctor said. "Not knowing the order in which they were fired, I couldn't determine which one actually killed the deputy."

"What was the caliber of the two bullets?"

"One was a .44, the other was a .31 caliber."

"I see. That means, then, does it not, that the other two bullets would not have proven fatal?"

"There's no way to actually determine that," Dr. Russell said. "Infectious gangrene could have caused either of the other bullets to be fatal."

"But, arriving on the scene as quickly as you did, do you not feel that you would have been able to save the deputy, if it had not been for the two fatal bullets?"

"Yes, I think I could have."

"Doctor, both Mr. Minner and Mr. Thatcher were armed with .31-caliber pistols. Which of their pistols fired the fatal shot?"

"Well, I...I don't know," the doctor said. "There's no way of telling that."

"In fact, there is, Doctor. There is a new technique, recently developed as a result of police investigation procedures in the East, by which it can be determined which gun fires which bullet."

"Perhaps so, but we have no such ability here," the doctor replied.

"Then you cannot say which of my two clients fired the fatal shot?"

"No, I cannot."

"Thank you, Doctor."

Later, during his summation to the jury, Foster Smith made much of the fact that no one could tell, with certainty, which of his two clients actually fired the fatal bullet.

"One of my clients is guilty of murder," he told the jury. "The other is guilty of bank robbery, but he is not guilty of murder. Which one is it? That is something we may never know, gentlemen, and because the law requires that guilt can only be established if a jury is convinced, beyond reasonable doubt, then we may never know who fired the fatal bullet.

"That leaves us with a dilemma, gentlemen, for we

cannot hang an innocent man. Our justice system is designed to protect the innocent. It is better to let the guilty man live...than to put to death an innocent man.

"Also, let us not forget that there was a third party involved in this business, and he was using a .44-caliber pistol. He was the only one using a .44-caliber pistol, and, as we know from Dr. Russell's testimony, one of the .44-caliber bullets could have been the fatal shot. That man, Leo McCoury, has already paid the supreme penalty for his action since he was killed in the process of his apprehension.

"That means, then, that Deputy Santos has been avenged. However, we are an enlightened people, and we know that it is not the purpose of the court to exact vengeance...it is the purpose of the court to seek justice. But there can be no justice if an innocent man is hanged. And since we do not know which of these two men fired the bullet which could have been fatal, we cannot determine with any certainty which one of them should be hanged. Therefore, the spirit of true justice, gentlemen of the jury, demands that we spare them both. My clients admit their guilt to the charge of bank robbery. Find them guilty of that, and assess the penalty such a crime demands. But, in the name of humanity, enlightenment, and yes, justice, I ask that you return a verdict of 'not guilty' to the charge of murder."

Foster Smith's closing argument was most impassioned, but the prosecutor was also a man of persuasive logic.

"It doesn't matter which one fired the fatal bullet,"

he told the jury. "Both of these men fired at Deputy Santos with the intent to kill. The learned and capable counsel for the defense is suggesting that because one of these two men is less proficient in the use of a firearm than the other, then he should be found not guilty of murder. But I would remind the jury that any unlawful death which might occur during the commission of a felony is to be considered murder in the first degree, and said guilt should fall equally upon all perpetrators. Armed bank robbery, gentlemen, is a felony, which means the unlawful death of Deputy Santos is murder in the first degree...to be shared equally by all perpetrators. Both Olie Minner and Bert Thatcher have admitted to the crime of bank robbery; therefore, they stand condemned by their own words."

The jury retired to the cloakroom to decide the case. They returned fifteen minutes later with a verdict of guilty on both counts, for both defendants.

Judge Whitmore heard the verdict, then cleared his throat and looked over at the sheriff.

"Sheriff Jenson, would you position the prisoners before the bench for sentencing, please?"

"Yes, Your Honor."

The two men were brought before the bench, where they stood with their heads bowed contritely.

"Mr. Minner and Mr. Thatcher, as I am sure you would both testify, you have had a fair and honest hearing. In fact, I would like to publicly compliment your attorney, Mr. Smith, for what I thought was a very good defense. Nevertheless, the jury, having heard all the testimony and all the arguments from both sides, has found you guilty. Therefore it is my unpleasant duty to sentence both of you to be hanged by the neck until you are dead. This sentence will be carried out at two o'clock in the afternoon, one week from today."

FIVE

"Hey you, prisoner, wake up," Bucky called.

Eli opened his eyes and saw that he was lying in a jail cell. At first he didn't understand how he got there, then he realized that he had gotten very drunk the night before.

"Ohh," he groaned, putting his hand to his head as he sat on the bunk. "Was I that drunk?" He looked around the cell. "Where's Poke and Lanny?"

"They're pushin' up daisies by now."

"Pushin' up daisies?" he asked in confusion. "What do you mean?"

"I mean they're deader'n a doornail," Bucky said, laughing.

It wasn't until that moment that Eli remembered the scene from the night before, seeing his two friends lying in pools of blood on the barroom floor. He jumped up quickly and ran to the door of his cell, wrapping his fingers around the steel bars.

"I've got to get out of here!" he shouted. "I've got to get back to the ranch and tell Mr. Howard."

Bucky was a very large man, and Eli remembered now that this was the one who'd brought him to jail last night.

"Bucky," Eli said. "Your name is Bucky, ain't it?"

"Not to you, it ain't," Bucky replied. "To you, it's Deputy Zorn."

"Deputy Zorn, I have to get out of here. How much is my fine? When can I pay it?"

Bucky laughed. "Fine? That's funny, mister. That's 'bout the funniest thing I ever heard. I ain't never heard of no one payin' a fine for murder."

"Murder? What are you talkin' about? I didn't murder anyone."

"You are in here for murder, boy. You, and them other two galoots that was with you, killed Deputy Collins last night."

"Why, I...I did no such thing," Eli said. "I was upstairs with a whore when all that happened. If you'll let me go over to the saloon, I'll find her an' she'll tell you."

"You ain't goin' nowhere," Bucky said. "You're goin' to have your trial right here, soon as the sheriff comes in."

"The sheriff? What about the judge?"

"Don't you know, boy? In Rebel Ridge, Sheriff Lowman is the judge."

Groaning, Eli walked back over to his bunk and sat down, holding his head in his hands. He was still in that position a few minutes later when he heard Bucky speak again.

"Stand up, boy," Bucky said. "Your trial's about to begin."

"Where?"

"Right here, in the jailhouse," Bucky said. "It saves lots of time."

"This ain't no courtroom," Eli said. "And this ain't no trial."

"If I say it's a trial, it's a trial," a new voice said. The speaker had a pockmarked face and a droopy, black mustache. He pulled up a chair and sat down.

"You're Sheriff Lowman, ain't you?" Eli asked.

"I'm Sheriff Lowman when I'm sheriffin'," Lowman answered. "I'm Judge Lowman when I'm judgin'. These here men, who are my deputies, are goin' to act as the jury."

Eli looked toward the front of his cell and saw that, in addition to Bucky, there were six men. All were wearing badges.

"Deputies can't be the jury, can they?" Eli asked.

"They can in my court."

"They's only six of 'em."

"That's all we need in my court. Now, you're charged with the murder of Deputy Slim Collins. How do you plead?"

"I didn't kill nobody!" Eli insisted.

"Maybe you didn't, but you come into town with them two boys and that makes you guilty of aidin' and abettin' a murder."

"Wait a minute! Don't I get a lawyer?"

"You got enough money for a lawyer?"

"Yes, I've got ten dollars here in my—" Eli began feeling around in his pockets and soon realized that he had no money at all. "My money," he said. "It's gone. Someone took my money."

"Then you can't afford a lawyer," Lowman replied. "Which means the court'll have to appoint one for you. Bucky, you are his lawyer."

"All right, Judge," Bucky said, smiling broadly.

"Now, how do you plead?"

"I plead not guilty," Eli said.

Lowman held up his hand. "You've got a lawyer now, boy. He'll plead for you. Counselor, how do you plead for your client?"

"I plead him guilty, Your Honor," Bucky said without consulting with Eli.

Lowman turned toward the six "jurors" and said, "You've heard the counselor for the defendant plead this here prisoner guilty. How do you find?"

"We find the sonofabitch guilty, Judge," one of the jurors said.

Using his pistol as a gavel, Lowman brought it down sharply on the table. "Boy, this court finds you guilty and sentences you to hang. Get him out there to the tree, boys, and let's get this over with," he said.

"Wait a minute!" Eli said. "You mean you're takin' me out to hang right now? I don't get no chance to appeal to a higher court?"

Lowman and the others laughed.

"Boy, there ain't no higher court in Rebel Ridge," Bucky said.

* * *

WHEN MRS. PUTNAM went into the Barnet General Mercantile Store that morning, she knew nothing of what had taken place in the Silver Strike Saloon the night before or of the "trial" that had just been conducted down in the sheriff's office a few minutes earlier. She knew only that George Barnet was expecting a new shipment of yarn and she wanted to see if it had arrived.

"Mama, would you buy me a stick of horehound candy?" her seven-year-old son, Eddie, asked.

"No," Mrs. Putnam said. "It will spoil your dinner. You just be a good boy and stay out of things while I look around."

Disappointed, Eddie walked over to look through the front window of the store.

"Good morning, Mrs. Putnam," George Barnet said, smiling broadly. "I'll just bet you are here to check on that yarn, aren't you?"

"Yes, did it come in?"

"It did, I'm happy to say. It arrived on yesterday's train. Why don't you let Mrs. Barnet show it to you?"

"Thank you."

"Mama," Eddie called.

"Not now, Eddie."

"Mama, there are a bunch of men out there around that big tree."

"Not now, Eddie. Can't you see I'm busy?"

Mrs. Putnam was too interested in looking at the skeins of colorful yarn to pay any attention to Eddie, but George Barnet looked up when Eddie mentioned several men around a tree. Curious as to what might be going on, he walked over to look through the window.

"Oh, my god," he said.

"What is it, George?"

"That's Sheriff Lowman and his deputies. They're fixin' to hang someone."

"Eddie!" Mrs. Putnam said. "Eddie, you get away from that window!"

"I want to watch, Mama," Eddie replied.

"You get away from that window right now, you hear me?" Mrs. Putnam ordered, coming over to grab her son by the shoulder.

"George," Mrs. Barnet said. "George, can't you do something?"

Barnet looked at his wife with a helpless expression on his face. "What do you propose that I do, woman?" he asked. "Go out there and single-handedly stop them?"

"Yes. No. I mean, I don't know. But we can't just stand by and let this happen, can we?"

"I'll...I'll go out and see if I can find out what's goin' on," Barnet said.

When Barnet stepped out onto the boardwalk in front of his store, he saw Jarred Littlefield and Doc Frazer standing there, watching the proceedings. Their faces were contorted in horror and impotent rage.

"Jarred, what is this?" Barnet asked, pointing toward the tree. "What's goin' on over there?"

"Didn't you hear the gunshots down at the saloon last night?" Littlefield asked.

"I suppose I did," Barnet said. "But there are

gunshots pert' near every night. I didn't pay no mind to 'em."

"These gunshots were different," Littlefield said. "Collins got himself killed."

"Collins? Slim Collins?" Barnet looked around before he spoke again. "Well, I can't say that he's any great loss." He looked over at a young man, who was standing alongside a buckboard, his arms tied to his side. "Is that the one who killed him?"

"No. The one who killed him is dead."

"Well, who's this, then?"

"His name is Eli Underhill," Doc Frazer said. "He's a cowboy from the Bar-H spread. He and two of his friends came in for a little fun last night. Things got out of hand...there was a shootout, Collins and the other two cowboys are dead, and they're about to hang this boy."

"You mean they're goin' to lynch him? No trial or anything?"

"Oh, he had a trial all right," Littlefield said. "If you can call it that. Sheriff Lowman held it down in the jail this mornin'."

"Lowman is the sheriff, not the judge."

"You want to go tell him that?" Littlefield asked.

Barnet didn't answer, though the expression on his face showed that he had no desire to confront Jesse Lowman.

"The boy would've been better off if he had been killed in the shootout along with his two friends," Barnet said.

"He wasn't in the shootout," Littlefield said.

"What do you mean he wasn't in the shootout? I

thought you said he was with the other two," Barnet said.

"He rode into town with them," Littlefield said. "But from what I hear, he was upstairs with one of Newberry's whores when all the shootin' started."

"He was? You mean he didn't have anything to do with the shootin' at all?"

"Nope."

"Oh, my god! Then this is nothing but murder," Barnet said.

"That's exactly what it is," Doc Frazer agreed. "We are about to witness a murder."

The three men watched helplessly as the young cowboy was helped up onto the back of the buckboard. Lowman stepped up to the prisoner then, holding a hood. He offered the hood to the young cowboy.

"No," Eli said, turning his head to one side. "When I meet my Maker, I want Him to see my face so that He may judge me innocent of any wrongdoin'."

"Have it your own way," Lowman growled. "You got 'ny last words?"

Eli looked out over the crowd. In the faces of those closest to the buckboard he saw an almost eager anticipation. In the faces of those farther back, he saw pity, sorrow, even shame. Nowhere did he see a face that offered hope.

"I reckon not," Eli replied.

"Come on, Jesse, get it over with," one of the deputies shouted. "I want to see him dance."

Lowman held up his hand, then stepped toward the edge of the buckboard to shout his words to those who had already gathered and those who were now gathering to see what was going on: "I want it known by ever'body present that this here is a legal hangin', the prisoner havin' been tried an' found guilty in a court of law."

"A court of law," Doc Frazer snorted under his breath. "There have been *lynchings* with more legal justification than this."

Though Doc Frazer spoke only loudly enough for Barnet and Littlefield to hear him, Lowman must have sensed that he said something, for he looked, challengingly, toward the three men.

"How about any of you three men over there?" Lowman called. "Have you anything to say on behalf of the prisoner?"

"If we did have anything to say, would it make any difference?" Littlefield asked.

"It would have no bearin' on the decision of this court," Lowman replied.

"Then we have nothing to say," Littlefield said.

Lowman looked over at Bucky and nodded. Bucky put the thirteen-knot noose around Eli's neck. When that was done, Lowman turned to the prisoner. "Boy, I'm tellin' you this for your own good. Whenever the buckboard is pulled out from under you, if you'll let your neck be relaxed, it'll snap like a twig and ever'thing will be over in a second. Tighten up and it's likely to take a little longer. I've seen men tighten up their neck, then kick for near half an hour after they was hung."

Though Eli said nothing, he did nod in the affirmative.

Lowman and Bucky jumped down from the buck-board. Lowman looked toward the front of the buck-board where the driver was sitting holding the reins of the team. Lowman nodded and the driver snapped the reins against the team, urging them forward. The buckboard pulled out from under Eli Underhill and the crowd gasped as he was dragged off by the rope. He fell a short distance, and then the rope stopped short. Perhaps Eli had taken Lowman's advice, for he didn't kick when he hit the bottom of the fall. In fact, except for the pendulum-like swing, there was no movement at all.

Six

Late in the afternoon, two new men came riding into town, whooping and shouting and firing their pistols into the air. As always under such circumstances, the long-suffering citizens of Rebel Ridge could do nothing but shiver in fear and resignation and pull back even deeper into their homes and businesses where they were taking refuge. How much longer, they wondered, could they bear up under such oppression?

From the second floor of the Barnet General Mercantile Store, Jarred Littlefield pulled the window shade to one side and looked down at the two new arrivals.

"What is it?" someone asked.

"It's nothing. Just a couple of riders comin' into town," Littlefield replied. "They are new men, I think. At least, I haven't seen them before. They're just shootin' into the air."

"Even that is dangerous," George Barnet complained. "A couple of weeks ago, I had to replace a windowpane in this very room because one of those wild men started shootin' into the air."

"Be glad it was just a windowpane," one of the others said.

"Yes, but what if my wife or one of my children had been in here?" Barnet asked.

"George is right. A man ought to be safe in his own home or place of business," Jake Rankin said. "I'm tellin' you, we've got to do somethin'. It can't go on like this much longer."

"Well, now, gentlemen, that's why we're here," Littlefield said. "I mean, as far as I'm concerned, hangin' that innocent cowboy last week, then claimin' it was a legal act...that's the last straw."

Littlefield let the shade fall back in place, then returned to his chair to rejoin the others. Littlefield was the general manager of the Consolidated Mining Company. George Barnet was the owner of the Barnet General Mercantile Store. Besides Littlefield and Barnet, there were four other men present in the room, all legitimate businessmen and leading citizens of Rebel Ridge. They were: Jake Rankin, the town carpenter; Ed Kotulla, owner of a leather goods store; Parson Jorgenson, the town preacher; and the town doctor, Abe Frazer. As Littlefield had suggested, the six men were meeting to discuss the problems which had befallen their town and to try and seek some solution.

"Perhaps if we did nothing," Parson Jorgenson suggested.

"Nothing? By god, we've tried doing nothing, and it doesn't work," Kotulla said. "Excuse my language, Parson."

"No, that's not what I mean," the parson replied. "We haven't done nothing...I mean, actively done nothing."

"Parson, what in the Sam Hill are you talkin' about?" Littlefield asked.

"Well, why does anyone come to a town in the first place?" Parson Jorgenson asked. "They come to town for the goods and services a town provides. Food, clothing, saddles, guns and ammunition, beer, whiskey, haircuts—everything that civilization offers. Suppose we didn't offer any such thing here. Suppose we got every merchant to agree to shut down his business."

"For how long?" Barnet asked.

"For as long as it takes," Jorgenson replied. "When the outlaws can no longer get the things a town has to offer, perhaps they'll leave our town and go somewhere else."

"You mean be someone else's worry?" Littlefield asked.

"Well, yes, in a manner of speaking," Jorgenson admitted.

"Maybe the parson's got a point there," Rankin suggested. "Why not give it a try?"

"And what about the townspeople during that time?" Barnet asked. "I've got folks that depend on me. What are they supposed to do for food and clothing?"

"Yeah, and what about us merchants?" Kotulla asked. "How are we supposed to make a living?"

"I didn't say it would be easy," the parson said. "I just said it was a possibility."

"There's another thing to consider here. I've got three women who are expecting children," Doc Frazer said. "Now I know babies have been comin' into this world long before there were doctors, but it looks like Mrs. Jones is goin' to have a difficult birth. What if she starts to deliver? Am I just supposed to stand by and do nothing?"

"Well, no, of course not," the parson stammered. "I mean, I wouldn't expect you to just let someone die."

"Yes, but that's just it, don't you see?" Kotulla asked. "If we convince Newberry over at the saloon to close down now, when truth to tell he's makin' more money than he ever has before..."

"But let's be fair to Newberry," Rankin said quickly. "He told me the extra money he's makin' isn't even payin' for all the damage they're doin' over there... breakin' up the tables and chairs, bustin' out all the windows. I know all that's goin' on, because I've done a lot of repair work for him myself. He's as ready to have these men leave as any of us."

"Maybe so. But then that's all the more reason he needs the extra money he's makin'," Kotulla continued. "And if he sees Doc here still treatin' folks, then he's goin' to feel like he has the right to continue to run his saloon. No, sir, I don't think it's goin' to work."

"Then what *are* we goin' to do?"

"Did any of you hear what happened over in Copperfield last week?" Littlefield asked.

"What? You mean the bank holdup?" Barnet asked.

"Not just the bank holdup. It's what happened

after that I'm talkin' about. The three that did it were caught. One was killed, and the other two was brought in. They already been tried—a legal trial, I might add —and they're goin' to be hung tomorrow."

"How'd they bring 'em in so fast? Did they get up a posse? Is that what you think we should do?" Rankin asked. "Because if it is, I'm willin', but I don't know if we could get enough men who would be."

Littlefield shook his head. "No, they didn't use a posse," he said. "One man brought them in."

"One man? Who?"

"Dane Calder."

"Dane Calder? Say, ain't he that bounty hunter who chases down lots of men?" Rankin asked.

Littlefield nodded. "That's him."

"I've heard tell he's nothin' but a killer his own self," Barnet said.

"That may be," Littlefield agreed. "But from what ever'one says, he ain't never killed a man that didn't need killin'."

"Look here," Doc Frazer said. "Are you sayin' we should get this bounty hunter to come clean up our town?"

"I believe we should if we could."

"Do you think we can?"

"I don't know. Maybe if we made it worth his while, he would come," Littlefield said. "After all, that is what he does for a living. He collects money off bringin' in outlaws."

"Yes, but as far as I know, there's no bounty on any of these men. Leastwise, not enough of a bounty to make it worth his while."

"Maybe we could come up with the money ourselves," Littlefield suggested. "I think I can speak for Consolidated Mining when I say we will offer one thousand dollars. Now, if we could raise that much money from the rest of the town, that would be two thousand dollars. That seems to me like it would be a generous enough sum to persuade Mr. Calder to come to our rescue."

"I'm willin' to come up with two hundred fifty," Barnet said. "Kotulla, if you can raise two hundred fifty, I think we can get that much out of Newberry over at the saloon. That would only leave two hundred fifty for the whole rest of the town."

"Two hundred fifty is pretty dear for me right now," Kotulla complained. "Lowman come in and took a saddle yesterday that was worth a hundred fifty, easy. And you know what he give me for it? Twenty dollars. Twenty measly dollars and that's all. Hell, it cost me damn near that much just to have it shipped out here, let alone what it cost me to buy it."

"Well, what are you tellin' me, Kotulla? That you want stuff like that to keep on happenin'?"

Kotulla shook his head. "No, by god, I don't," he said. "All right, I'll come up with two hundred and fifty dollars. Parson, you think you could raise the rest from your parishioners?"

Parson Jorgenson shook his head. "Gentlemen, do you hear what you are saying? You are saying that you are willing to pay a hired killer to come to town to kill these men."

"You're damn right that's what we're sayin'," Rankin said.

"If we do that, it would make us no better than the men we are trying to eliminate, don't you see? We are resorting to the ways of violence."

"Yeah, well, Preacher, sometimes there just ain't no other way," Barnet said. "Not too many years back, you might recollect, this whole country was pushed into violence. We fought us one hell of a war to preserve the Republic. I was just a young man from Ohio then, but I picked up a soldier's pack and I went off to do my duty. I was an artilleryman at Shiloh, Preacher. I seen enough violence to last me a lifetime. And I didn't go through all that to kowtow to a bunch of varmints like Jesse Lowman and his gang. No, sir. If we have to pay someone to come kill 'em, then I say better them than us. Now, are you in or out?"

"I can't condone this," Parson Jorgenson said. He stood up and reached for his hat, then pulled it down low on his head. "Gentlemen, I will make no effort to stop you, or to get in your way. But, in all good conscience, I cannot actively take part in this. I won't solicit money for you, and I won't be a part of the committee that deems it necessary to employ a professional killer. If you'll excuse me?"

"I'm real sorry you feel that way, Parson Jorgenson," Littlefield said. "I think that now, more than any other time, a town needs the moral guidance of a preacher."

"Moral guidance?" Parson Jorgenson repeated. He sighed, and shook his head. "I thought that was what I just tried to offer you. Good day, gentlemen."

The others watched Jorgenson go down the stairs, then heard the door down on the street open and shut.

"Ah, the hell with him. We don't need him anyway," Barnet said.

"No, but it would have been good to have him support us," Littlefield said.

"Hell, we've only got two hundred fifty more dollars to raise. We can do it without him."

"It isn't just the money," Littlefield said. "His support would have lent a degree of moral credence to what we are plannin' to do. It would have gone a long way toward gettin' rid of any squeamishness some of the townspeople might have."

* * *

ACROSS THE STREET from the Barnet General Mercantile Store, the two men who had just ridden into town a few minutes earlier were now in the Silver Strike Saloon. One of them, drinking whiskey from a bottle, walked over to look out across the top of the batwing doors onto the street. He took a long swallow, then wiped his mouth with the back of his hand.

"Hey, Fontaine, get over here and look at this," he said, laughing. "This is about the funniest-lookin' thing I ever seen."

Fontaine, who also was drinking his whiskey from a bottle, was leaning against the bar.

"What you find so funny, Truitt?" Fontaine asked.

"The hat this here fella is wearin'. Come over here and take a gander at it."

Fontaine walked over to the batwing doors. "Where?" he asked.

"Hell, are you blind? It's right there," Truitt said.

"Look at the crown of that hat. Look how low down the crown of that hat is. Why, I bet it don't come up more'n two inches from the top of the head. And now look at how wide the brim is. You figure the fella that made that hat was drunk, or somethin'?"

"Naw, that fella's a preacher, that's all," Fontaine said. He took a drink of his whiskey then lowered the bottle. "Don't you see how he's all dressed in black, an' wearin' that funny collar? That's the kind of hats preachers sometimes wear."

"Hell, I know'd he was a preacher," Truitt said. "I was just makin' comment on the hat, is all." He took another drink. "Bet I could shoot it off his head."

"From how far?"

"From here."

Fontaine measured the distance between the door of the saloon and the approaching preacher.

"The hell, you say," he said. "That crown's no more'n two inches high, and he's a good two hundred and fifty feet away."

"It'd be a hell of a shot, I admit, but ten bucks says I can do it," Truitt insisted, taking out his pistol. "I'm just goin' to let him get a little closer."

"All right, I'll take that bet. But you see the other end of that water trough?" Fontaine said.

"Yeah, I see it. What about it?"

"That's too close. If you don't shoot it off before he gets there...the bet's off."

"Get your ten bucks ready," Truitt said, taking careful aim.

* * *

BACK IN THE loft of Barnet's Store, Jake Rankin, feeling a need to stretch his legs, had gotten up and moved over to the window. He was watching the preacher walk down the street. Behind him, he could hear the buzz of conversation as the others discussed how best to approach Dane Calder. They were trying to talk Doc Frazer into being the messenger, believing that he was the one to whom Calder would most likely listen. But Doc Frazer was having a difficult time being persuaded, because he was beginning to believe that perhaps Parson Jorgenson was right.

"How do we know we won't be jumpin' from the frying pan into the fire?" Doc asked the others. "Maybe this isn't such a good idea after all."

"Dammit, Doc, we've got to do somethin'," Barnet insisted.

Suddenly Rankin saw a flash and a puff of smoke emerge from just inside the saloon door. A second later, he heard the shot and, at almost the same time, saw the preacher go down. Jorgenson fell on his back with his arms stretched out in the dirt on either side of him. His hat was off, and his head was thrown back. Clearly visible, even from the second floor of Barnet's Store, was the large, bloody hole in the middle of Jorgenson's forehead.

"Oh, my god!" Rankin said.

The others looked toward him.

"What is it, Jake? What'd you just see?"

"They just shot the preacher," Rankin said in a quiet, tight voice.

"What?" Littlefield asked. He rushed over to the window, followed by the others.

"My god! Who did it?"

"I don't know exactly," Rankin said. "But I seen the puff of smoke. The shot come from inside the saloon."

Doc Frazer started quickly down the stairs.

"Doc, where you goin'?"

"To see if I can do anything for the preacher," Doc Frazer called back over his shoulder.

The others followed him down the stairs, then out into the street, though in truth, it was as much out of a sense of morbid curiosity as it was any desire to help. Actually, they already knew that the preacher was beyond help.

By the time they reached Jorgenson, there were already a couple of dozen people gathered around the grisly scene. The way Jorgenson was lying, with his arms spread straight out to either side of him, reminded Littlefield of Christ on the cross. He thought the symbolism was significant, though he didn't comment on it.

"Can you do anything for him, Doc?" Newberry asked.

Doc Frazer, who was squatted down beside the body, sighed and shook his head. "He was dead before he hit the ground," he said as he stood up. "What the hell happened? Who shot him, and why?"

"I reckon I done it," Truitt said.

"Who are you?" Doc asked.

"The name is Truitt. Felix Truitt. But I want you to know that it was an accident and I'm just real remorseful about it."

"An accident? An accident?" Doc Frazer said.

"Man, how do you accidentally shoot someone right between the eyes?"

"I bet Fontaine here ten dollars I could knock off his funny little hat," Truitt said. "I reckon I missed. I don't understand it, neither. I had me a real good bead on it."

"You bet ten dollars?" Doc Frazer said angrily. "You killed a man for ten dollars?"

"Take it easy, Doc," a new voice said. "You heard him say it was an accident."

When Doc Frazer looked around, he saw that Lowman and his chief deputy, Bucky, had come upon the scene. "Hello, Truitt, Fontaine," Lowman said. "I heard you boys was comin' to join us. It's good to see you."

Truitt and Fontaine shook Lowman's hand and smiled broadly. "Sonofabitch!" Truitt said. "It's true then, ain't it? You are the sheriff over here!"

"That's right," Lowman said. "I'm also the judge. And, as the judge, I owe it to the good people of this town to see that justice is done here." He pointed to the preacher's body. "I'm afraid you two men are goin' to have to pay for this."

"Now, wait a minute, Jesse," Truitt said. "I done told you it was an accident. And I told these here folks just how remorseful I am. Now that ought to be the end of it."

"Yeah, well, bein' sorry ain't quite enough," Lowman said. "I got to come up with some sort of penalty." He suddenly smiled. "I got it," he said. "What was it you said you was bettin'? Ten dollars?"

"Yeah, ten dollars."

"All right, that would make the pot a total of twenty dollars. I'll take it," Lowman said.

"Hold on, Jesse, that ain't hardly right," Fontaine said. "The money's mine now—I won the bet. Besides which, I didn't shoot the sonofabitch, Truitt did."

"You didn't shoot him but you...uh, what's that word?" Lowman asked. Then he smiled. "Oh, yeah, 'aided and abetted.' You aided and abetted this here accidental shootin', so you got to pay up just like Truitt here. I'll take the twenty dollars."

Grumbling, Fontaine handed over the twenty dollars. "It don't seem right," he said. "We told you it was an accident."

"Yeah, well, accident or not, the preacher's dead and he's goin' to need a decent buryin'," Lowman said. He took the twenty dollars from Fontaine, then handed it over to Doc Frazer. "I tell you what, Doc," Lowman said. "You take this here money and see to it the preacher gets buried real proper." Lowman brushed his hands together as if having just finished a difficult task. "There, now, that's all took care of, short and sweet. Come on back into the saloon, boys. I'll swear you in as my deputies, then we'll visit for a while."

When Lowman and his deputies left, there remained behind only those townspeople who were both curious enough and courageous enough to be out in the street.

"Deputies. Did you hear that?" someone asked disgustedly. "Lowman's goin' to make them two galoots deputies."

"Yeah, so what? They ain't no different from any of the others," another answered.

By now, the undertaker had also arrived, and he was looking down solemnly at the body.

"Will twenty dollars be enough to handle the buryin', Gus?" Doc Frazer asked, handing over the money.

Gus waved the money aside. "Jake was just tellin' me that you're goin' to be goin' around town, collectin' money to hire someone to come help us out," he said. "You go ahead an' put that twenty dollars in the pot. I'll bury Parson Jorgenson for free."

"What do you say, Doc?" Littlefield asked. "You still think the preacher was right?"

Doc Frazer took one last look at the preacher, then shook his head.

"Get the rest of the money together," he said. "I'll be your messenger."

SEVEN

WHEN DOC FRAZER RODE INTO THE LITTLE TOWN of Copperfield the next day, he thought they must be having a circus. The street was crowded with men, women, and children, most of whom were dressed in their Sunday finery. A medicine wagon was doing a brisk business at one end of the street, while else-where, vending kiosks had been set up to offer for sale sandwiches, beer, or candy.

"Annabel! Annabel, you get back here," an anxious mother called to a little girl who dashed out into the street. "Billy, go out there and get your sister!"

"Oh, Mom, Larry says he knows where there's a good spot in the loft of the livery. If I don't hurry, someone else will beat me to it," Billy complained.

"Go get your sister, I said," the mother repeated, undaunted by the young man's complaint. "You want her to get runned over?"

Doc drove his buckboard and team past the medi-cine wagon. There were several men and women gathered around the wagon, listening to the pitchman give his spiel.

"Hey, Professor!" someone shouted from the crowd. "Do you reckon a bottle of your tonic will do them boys any good after they get hung?"

The others laughed.

"My friend," the pitchman replied easily, "it might indeed, but far be it from me to thwart the intent of the law. No, sir, I do not intend to put it to the test."

The crowd laughed even harder.

A young towheaded boy hurried out to meet Doc's buckboard. He was holding up a paper.

"Mister, you want a souvenir program?" the boy asked. "They only cost a nickel."

Doc stopped his team. "Only a nickel?" He smiled at the boy. "Well, I guess I could afford one of those," he said, taking a coin from his pocket. "What is it a souvenir of?"

"Are you jokin' with me, mister?" the boy asked. "You mean you don't know about the double hangin' we're havin' here in Copperfield?"

"You mean that's what all this is?" Doc asked, taking in the crowd with a sweep of his hand. "All these people are here to see a hanging?"

"Sure. We ain't never had no hangin' here before," the boy said. "Leastwise, not one that was legal. They found Paul Blalock hangin' from a tree couple of months ago, but don't nobody know yet who done that. This here hangin' is all legal and proper. You can read all about it in the program," the boy added. He turned and started toward another part of the crowd.

"Program!" he shouted. "Get your souvenir program here!"

Doc looked at the program.

GALLOWS HANGING!
OF THE NOTED OUTLAWS
OLIE MINNER AND BERT THATCHER
TO TAKE PLACE IN THE TOWN OF
COPPERFIELD
ON TUESDAY, SEPTEMBER 21ST

SCHEDULE OF EVENTS:
ADDRESS BY
ARIZONA TERRITORIAL LIEUTENANT GOVERNOR
THE HONORABLE T. ELLSWORTH SHIPMAN
SONGS BY METHODIST CHURCH CHOIR
ADDRESS BY THE REVEREND FINIS W. TURNER
MUSIC BY THE COPPERFIELD VOLUNTEER FIRE
DEPARTMENT BAND
READING OF WARRANT OF EXECUTION BY
SHERIFF AARON JENSON
ORDER FOR EXECUTION TO COMMENCE BY
THE HONORABLE JUDGE JEREMIAH WHITMORE
PRAYER BY THE REVEREND FINIS W. TURNER
LAST WORDS BY OLIE MINNER AND BERT THATCHER
HANGING

DOC FRAZER CONTRASTED the organized structure of this legal hanging with the lynching he had witnessed

back in Rebel Ridge last week. The result of any hanging, be it legal or illegal, was the same, he knew. But
there was something reassuring in the organization and
structure of a legal hanging. Though he probably
couldn't have articulated his thoughts, he knew that
this structure offered some protection. Surely no one
would be hanged in such a fashion unless he had already
had the benefit of the fullest due process of law.

On the other hand, he thought, what happened in
Rebel Ridge last week could have happened to just
about anyone. Though he would not wish upon any
man the ordeal of witnessing a hanging, he couldn't
help but think it would be good if Barnet and Littlefield were over here now, so that they could see justice
being carried out as it was supposed to be.

Doc parked his buckboard in a lot where dozens of
other buckboards and wagons stood, then walked
across the crowded street to the sheriff's office. To one
side of the sheriff's building a couple of men were
putting the finishing touches on the newly constructed
gallows. A man who Doc figured must be the hangman
was sitting on the side of the gallows, working with a
rope. One rope had already been fashioned into a thirteen-knot noose and was lying, ominously, to one side.

There were a total of five men inside the building.
Three were gathered around a desk, laughing and talking. The other two, who were much more solemn,
were in the jail's only cell. These, Doc assumed, were
the condemned prisoners.

One of the three men around the desk looked up
when Doc Frazer came in.

"If you're lookin' for tickets to the hangin', you

don't need any," he said. Frazer saw that the man was wearing a badge on his vest. "Just go out there and find yourself a good place to stand."

"The street is so crowded now, I doubt there is anyplace to stand," one of the other men said.

The sheriff pointed to the cell. "Well, hell, that ain't no problem," he said. "I reckon either one of these boys would give up his place for you." He and the other two men around the desk laughed at his joke.

"I'm not here for the hanging," Doc Frazer said.

"You ain't?" the sheriff asked. "What are you here for?"

"My name is Dr. Abe Frazer. I live over in Rebel Ridge."

"Rebel Ridge," the sheriff snorted. "Then I can see why you ain't interested in a hangin'. From what I hear, you folks had a hangin' of your own over there, last week."

"Hanging? Lynching, you mean," Doc Frazer said.

"Lynching? That's a pretty strong charge," one of the men said. He was a short, fat man wearing a three-piece suit with a gold watch chain stretched across the vest.

"Who are you?" Doc Frazer asked.

"I am Judge Whitmore."

"Lynching may be a strong word, Judge, but it is, nonetheless, an accurate representation of what happened," Doc Frazer said. "By the way, I understand it was Dane Calder who brought these men in. Is that correct?"

"That's right."

"Good, then I'm not too late. I suppose he's out there, somewhere, waiting for the hanging?"

"May I inquire as to why you are interested in Calder?" Judge Whitmore asked.

"It is my hope...rather, it is the hope of myself and several others in our community that Mr. Calder can be persuaded to come to Rebel Ridge to, uh, bring peace to our town."

"Evidently, that's what you tried to do last week," Judge Whitmore said. "Bring peace to your town by hanging—or, as you suggest, by lynching—an outlaw."

"An outlaw? Judge, that boy was no more of an outlaw than I am," Doc said. "None of them were. They were just cowboys, that's all, come to town for a little relaxation. One of Lowman's deputies goaded two of them into a fight and they were killed. The boy they hanged was upstairs at the time. He didn't have anything to do with it."

"Then you do have a bad situation over there, I admit," Judge Whitmore said. "I wish my jurisdiction extended that far, but I would have to get the approval from the federal court to come over there and intervene. And, I would have to have the support of the local sheriff."

"Lowman?"

"He is the sheriff."

"He is also the biggest problem."

"Then you see my dilemma," Judge Whitmore said.

"And you see ours. That's why I've come to speak with Mr. Calder."

"Well, you won't find Calder out there," Judge Whitmore said. "He never watches the hangings."

"You mean I've missed him?"

The judge shook his head. "No, I didn't say that. I just said you won't find him watching the hanging. In fact, I know he's still in town. He's waiting for the reward money to come through."

"Where is he? Has he taken a hotel room somewhere?"

"I think he has," the sheriff offered. "But you'll most likely find him over at the saloon."

"Thanks," Doc said.

The saloon was across the street and several buildings down the block. Doc pushed his way through the crowd then stepped up onto the boardwalk. How total the town's fascination was with the upcoming hanging was especially evident in the saloon, as it was almost completely empty. None of the lanterns were lit, and the interior was lighted only by the alternating bars of light and shadow which stabbed in through the slits in the window shutters and splashed in over the batwing doors.

Over in the shadows behind the bar, a lone bartender stood, busily polishing glasses. In the darkest gloom of the farthest corner of the saloon there was another man, a single customer who was sitting at a table, staring into his glass. The customer looked up as Doc approached his table.

"Mr. Calder?" he asked.

"Dane will do."

Doc pointed to one of the chairs around the table. "Do you mind if I join you?"

The chair slid out in invitation, and Doc saw that Dane had pushed it out with his foot.

"Thank you."

"You have the money?" Dane asked.

"Yes," Doc said. "How did you...? Oh, you mean the reward money for the two men who are about to be hanged, don't you? Uh, no, I don't have it."

"What money are you talking about?"

"I, uh, have a proposition for you, Dane," Doc said.

Dane took a swallow of his drink and studied Doc over the rim of his glass. "What sort of proposition?" he asked, putting the glass back down.

"My name is Dr. Abe Frazer. I represent the good citizens of Rebel Ridge," Doc said. "Have you ever heard of it?"

"Yeah, I've heard of it."

"We used to mine silver in Rebel Ridge," Doc said. "When that played out, we switched to copper. In a lot of ways, that was even better. Copper tends to attract more solid citizens than gold or silver. At least that was what we thought. Instead, Rebel Ridge is hell on earth. There are beatings and frequent killings. Decent men are being cheated and robbed of their stores and businesses. The good people are too frightened to leave their homes. We are being turned into a ghost town by a bunch of outlaws."

"Go to the sheriff," Dane suggested.

Doc shook his head. "You don't understand. The sheriff and his deputies *are* the outlaws. Why, they lynched an innocent man last week, then tried to pass it off as a legal hanging."

Dane took another swallow of his drink. "Why are you comin' to me with this?"

"Well I—that is, we—thought you might be willing to help us if, uh, the price was right. I don't know exactly what your price is, Mr. Calder. But we have raised two thousand dollars. The money is for you if you will…"

"Kill the sheriff and his deputies?" Dane asked.

"Well, no, not exactly."

"Then what, exactly?" Dane asked. "You know these men. If they have a good thing goin' over there in Rebel Ridge, and it sounds to me like they do, do you think they are goin' to just go away?"

"Probably not," Doc admitted.

"And if they don't go away, how am I supposed to take care of the situation?"

"I don't know," Doc said.

In the streets outside the saloon, the crowd noises had stopped and there could now be heard the shouted words of someone making a speech:

"*A code of justice…and decent, God-fearing, law-abiding men to administer that justice…*"

Dane finished his drink. "The only way I could take care of it would be to kill the sheriff and as many of his deputies as it took to get the others to leave," he said. "Am I right?"

"Yes," Doc said quietly.

"I want to get this straight, Doc," Dane said. "I want you to understand that you and the 'good' citizens of Rebel Ridge are attemptin' to hire me to kill for you."

"I…I guess if you want to put it like that."

"How else should I put it?"

"No way else, I guess."

The speech was over outside, and now a choir was singing hymns:

> *Oh worthy Judge eternal!*
> *When Thou dost bid us come,*
> *Then open wide the gates of pearl,*
> *And call Thy servants home.*

Dane smiled, though the smile never reached his eyes. "Well, I'll save your conscience for you," he said. "I won't do it."

"You...you won't accept the job?"

"That's what I said."

"Why not? Is it not enough money? Because if that's the problem, maybe we can raise more. How much more do we need?"

"It isn't the money," Dane said. "I'm not a hired killer."

"But you...you are a bounty hunter, aren't you?" Doc asked.

"A bounty hunter, Doc, not a bounty killer," Dane said. "I've killed when I've had to. I bring them in when I can. What's going on outside should be proof of that."

The hymns were over now, and another speech was in progress:

"*...to bring law to the lawless, and to take our place, in dignity, upon the stage of man.*"

"What *is* goin' on outside?" Doc asked. "The men you brought in alive are about to be killed, aren't they? What difference did it make whether you did it or whether it is done by the law? They are just as dead. In fact, given their choice, they would probably rather they had been killed by you. That way, at least they wouldn't have had to go through this macabre circus."

Dane nodded. "I'll grant that you have a point there," he said. "They probably would have been better off." He sighed. "But that isn't my decision to make." He got up and walked over toward the bar to pour himself another drink.

Now, from outside, there was band music.

"Listen, Dane, do you think it's easy for me to come to you with this proposition?" Doc called over to him. "I'm a doctor, for God's sake. Do you know what that means? That means I have spent my entire life tryin' to save others. And now, here I am, offerin' you blood money to kill other human beings. My god, man, this is a violation of all that I believe in, of every-thing that I hold dear. But, I swear to you, sir, if ever there was a man who needed killin', it is Jesse Lowman."

Dane looked back around quickly. "Did you say Jesse Lowman?"

"Yes," Doc said. "We—that is, the Consolidated Mining Company—hired him to guard the silver ship-ments back when they were still mining silver. When they switched from silver to copper, they no longer had need of his services, so they let him go. Only, he didn't leave town. Instead he browbeat the city council into making him the sheriff. It has been hell since then."

The band music stopped.

Dane turned back to the bar and raised the glass to his mouth. "I don't know who it was, but it was a wise man who once said that most men create their own hell. I suppose that is true for towns, too."

"All right, all right, I'll admit, we brought Jesse Lowman into town," Doc Frazer said. "But should everyone suffer for that? The women and children, the innocent? Dane, you don't know what we've been goin' through."

"I'm sorry," Dane said. "I can't help you."

During their last few exchanges, there were a few more words audible from outside, concluding with these:

"...hanged by the neck until dead."

"Then, if there is nothing I can do to change your mind...?" Doc said in one final plea.

"Nothing," Dane said. By now, Dane had turned his back to the doctor and stood at the bar, staring morosely into his drink.

"I'll be goin' then." Doc looked pointedly at Dane for a long moment, but Dane never bothered to look around. Outside the preacher was saying a final prayer for the condemned:

"Unto God's gracious mercy and protection we commit thee. The Lord bless thee, and keep thee. The Lord make his face to shine upon thee, and be gracious unto thee. The Lord lift up his countenance upon thee, and give thee peace, both now and evermore. Amen."

After Doc left the saloon he pushed his way through the crowd. It was strangely silent now, compared to the earlier circus atmosphere. One of the outlaws had just been invited to speak. Doc looked around and saw him standing there with his arms bound stiffly by his sides and his legs tied together.

"As I look around here," the outlaw said, "I see very many enemies and very few friends. You youngsters, when you grow old, remember me to your grandchildren. Those memories of me are all that will be left of Olie Minner."

The other outlaw declined the invitation to speak. Doc found his buckboard, then turned his team around and started out of the lot, keeping the activity in the street behind him. A moment later, he heard the thumping sound of the trapdoors falling open, then the collective gasp of the crowd. After that, there was a moment of silence.

Doc knew the two men were now swinging silently from the ends of the ropes, but he made no effort to look around to see them. Instead, he rode to the far end of the street, then turned onto the road leading back to Rebel Ridge. Not once did he look back.

EIGHT

IT WAS AFTER DARK BY THE TIME DOC RETURNED TO Rebel Ridge. He could hear the town even before he saw it—the trill of a piano, the breaking of glass, then a woman's high-pitched scream, followed by a man's basso laughter. These were the sounds of a town in its death throes, and Doc slumped down in his seat as he let the team plod along over the familiar trail. As he drew closer, he could see the shine of lights from the saloons.

Wearily and dejectedly, he headed for the livery stable. As he pulled his team to a stop, he heard someone call to him from the shadows.

"Doc?"

"Who is it?" Doc asked, staring into the darkness.

"It's me, Littlefield," Littlefield said, walking into a little patch of light thrown by the lantern on the front of the stable. "I thought I'd wait for you to come back. The others are over at Barnet's waitin' for me to bring you over."

Doc sighed. "I wish I had somethin' to bring them," he said.

"Didn't you find Calder?"

"Oh, yes, I found him all right," Doc said. "But it didn't do any good. He won't help us."

"Why not? Is it not enough money? Look, Doc, if we have to raise more money, we can do it. I'll write a letter to the mine owners, explainin' what's goin' on around here. In a way, it's the mine's fault anyway. If we hadn't hired Lowman in the first place, none of this would be happenin' now."

"I wish I could tell you that more money is all we need," Doc said.

"But that isn't it. Calder won't do it, no matter how much money we offer him." Doc began unhitching his team and Littlefield helped.

"Why not?" Littlefield asked from his side of the team.

"He says what we're doin' is offering to pay him to be our killer."

"Yeah, I guess it is," Littlefield said. "What's wrong with that?"

"What's wrong with that is Calder doesn't consider himself a hired killer."

"What the hell does he consider himself?"

"A bounty hunter," Doc said.

"Hell, ever'body knows there ain't no difference between a bounty hunter and a hired killer."

"Evidently, there is a difference," Doc said. "Perhaps to us, it is a subtle difference, but to Calder, it is very real." By now the team was unhitched, and Doc and Littlefield turned them into the corral. Both horses went immediately to the hayrick, where they began feeding. "I don't know," Doc added. "Maybe Calder is right. Maybe we have no business hirin' someone to kill for us."

"Come on, let's get over to Barnet's to see the others," Littlefield said. "They're waiting to hear from us, but I'm sure not lookin' forward to tellin' 'em what you found out."

As the two men walked across the dark street, headed for the mercantile store, Fontaine, who had been in the shadows all along, spit out his chew of tobacco, then wiped his mouth. When Doc and Little-field were far enough out into the dark so he couldn't be seen, he started toward the Silver Strike. He was pretty sure Lowman would want to hear this.

The saloon was lit by one huge, bright chandelier, as well as by a dozen or so kerosene lanterns. The bar was crowded, and the tables were full. At least half a dozen of the men were wearing the badges of deputy. The others, while not officially deputies, were never-theless taking advantage of the "wide-open" condi-tions of the town. Some, Fontaine knew, were petty criminals, not well enough known to have to be on the run but unable, or unwilling, to adjust to conditions in a normal town. Rebel Ridge was perfect for them. Here, there was no such thing as disturbing the peace or public drunkenness.

Jesse Lowman was sitting at a table in the back corner of the saloon. He called this table his "office," and no one could sit at it without his express invita-tion. There were three others at his table now—a bar girl who had pulled her chair so close to his that her leg was lying across his lap and two men, both of whom were studying the cards they were holding.

"Are you boys goin' to bet, or are you just goin' to sit there twiddlin' your thumbs?" Lowman asked.

"I'm foldin'," one of the men said, throwing his cards in.

"Yeah, me too," the other followed. He, too, laid down his cards.

"Damn," Lowman said, raking in the pot. "You boys don't even make it fun." He looked up at Fontaine. "What about you, Fontaine? You want to play?"

"I ain't got enough money yet," Fontaine answered.

"Well then, what are you doin' over here?"

"I heard somethin' a while ago that I thought you might want to know," Fontaine said.

"What's that?"

"Did you know the townspeople has got themselves together and raised enough money to hire 'em a bounty hunter?" Fontaine asked. "I think they wanted him to come to town and run us out."

Lowman chuckled. "Just one bounty hunter? They must think he's one hell of a man." He had shuffled the cards and was beginning to redeal.

"They was talkin' like he was," Fontaine said. "But he can't be too much. Leastwise, I ain't never heard of the sonofabitch."

"Who is it?" Lowman asked.

"Somebody named Calder."

Lowman stopped dealing and looked squarely at Fontaine. "Who did you say?"

"Somebody named Calder," Fontaine repeated. "I

didn't get his first name. Anyhow, it don't matter. He's not comin'." Fontaine chuckled. "I reckon he showed yellow."

"I've heard Dane Calder called lots of things," Lowman said. "But I've never heard him called yellow."

Frank Colby was playing cards at a nearby table, and he chuckled. "You afraid of Dane Calder are you, Lowman?"

"You aren't?"

"Nope," Colby said easily. He took the makings from his shirt pocket and began rolling a cigarette. "I figure he puts on his pants pert' near like anyone else."

"It ain't the way he puts on his pants that makes him dangerous," Lowman said.

"Well, don't be frightened, Lowman," Colby said smugly. "If you want me to, I'll take care of Calder for you."

The other deputies laughed nervously, and Lowman glared at Colby.

"Oh, I'm not frightened, Colby," Lowman said. "I don't plan to go out of my way to run across him, but I'm not frightened."

"Maybe you think you can't beat him," Colby said, licking the cigarette paper, then tamping it closed. "I know I can."

"Colby, when you talk like that...it makes it sound as if you think you can beat me."

Colby lit his cigarette and then squinted through the cloud of smoke.

"I can," he said.

There was a sudden scraping of tables and chairs as everyone moved out of the way of the two men.

"Do you want to try right now?" Lowman asked coldly, calmly.

Colby had faced many men, but he was used to seeing fear in their eyes and was always able to use that fear to his advantage. Lowman, however, was showing absolutely no fear whatever...and that lack of fear gave Colby pause. For the first time in his life, he had an inkling of what others must feel. He wasn't exactly afraid of Lowman...but he didn't have total confidence that he would come out the better in any encounter between the two of them.

Slowly, deliberately, he took a puff from his cigarette, forcing himself to remain calm. He smiled insincerely.

"Now, why would I want to do something like that?" he asked. "You're the sheriff here, and I've got a good thing goin' bein' your deputy. Besides that, I always figured we were friends. Friends don't go around throwin' down on friends, do they?"

"Colby, sometimes you have a funny way of talkin' to your friends," Lowman said.

Colby forced a chuckle. "Well he said. "You might say that I'm a funny kind of guy."

During the exchange of words between Lowman and Colby, the music and laughter stopped, and the loud conversation stilled. Lowman now noticing the quiet, spoke out loud.

"What is it?" Lowman asked. "What's got into ever'one?"

"Nothin', Jesse," Bucky said. "Nothin' at all."

"Well, get on back to your drinkin' an' card playin'. There ain't nothing about to happen here that I can't handle."

"Yeah," Colby added. "Me an' Jesse was just havin' a friendly conversation about Dane Calder that's all."

"I been meanin' to ask, Jesse. Just who is this guy anyway?" Bucky inquired. "I mean, he's just one man, ain't he?"

"Colby, you keep talkin' about Calder like maybe you have his number. Let me ask you this. Have you ever tangled with him?" Lowman asked.

"No," Colby admitted. "I don't reckon anyone has who has lived to tell the tale. That's what makes him such a bogeyman."

"I know someone who has tangled with him...and who has lived to tell the tale," Lowman said.

"Who?"

"Me."

"You?" Colby asked. "I thought you were saying you didn't want to run across him again."

"I don't, particularly," Lowman answered. "You ever hit a hornets' nest with a stick?"

Colby chuckled. "Can't say as I have."

"Well, if you were ever to do that once, you'd have more sense than to do it again," Lowman said. "That's what I did with Calder. I hit a hornets' nest with a stick."

"What happened?"

"What happened was, I shot him once, but I didn't finish him off," Lowman said. "I left him out there for the buzzards, only the buzzards threw him back."

"You...you mean you beat him?" Colby asked, visibly impressed by Lowman's revelation.

"I didn't exactly beat him," Lowman admitted. "I shot the sonofabitch from ambush."

"Why didn't you finish him off?"

"I knew that I only hurt him," Lowman said. "Some creatures, like bears, mountain lions, and Dane Calder, you don't get close to when they're just wounded."

"What are you goin' to do if he comes?" Colby asked. "You're goin' to have to get close to him."

"He ain't comin'," Lowman said.

"He ain't? I thought that's what all this was about."

"That's 'cause you listened with your ass instead of your ears," Lowman growled. "Tell him, Fontaine."

"I overheard the doctor and another fella talkin' down at the livery a little while ago," Fontaine said. "Seems like they sent for Calder and they tried to pay him to come, but he wouldn't do it."

"Hell no, he wouldn't do it," Wooten, another deputy, said. "He's afraid of Lowman!"

"Yeah! Let's hear it for Lowman!" Bucky said.

All the deputies cheered then, except for Colby, who took a drink of his beer.

"Lowman, you got my vote to be sheriff as long as you want the job," one of the other deputies said.

"I don't need your vote, Simmons," Lowman said dryly. "Hell, I voted for myself. That's all the vote I need."

While the others laughed uproariously, Colby took a final puff from his cigarette.

NINE

IT WAS NEARLY NOON THE NEXT DAY, AND FELIX Truitt had been dry all morning. He wanted a drink, but he didn't have any money and that created a problem. If he had wanted to eat, all he would have had to do would be to go into the Railroad Café and order it with a promise to "pay later." His deputy's badge gave him that authority. There were any number of other goods and services he could "purchase" in town with the promise to pay later just because he was one of Lowman's deputies.

Those privileges did not extend to whiskey or beer, though, because Lowman had made himself a partner in the saloon. Lowman got a cut from every drink that was sold, which meant the drinks had to be sold for cash to everyone, including the deputies.

That was the bad side. The good side was that it wasn't very difficult for a deputy to get money...at least enough money to buy a drink. All he had to do was collect a little "personal tax." This personal tax was the only way the deputies had of being paid, and they were responsible for collecting it themselves. When Lowman had set up that system, he'd also explained how it was to work.

"If you take everything they have at the point of a gun," Lowman had told his deputies, "it would be robbery. But if you only take a small amount, it will be taxation, and the citizen will be grateful for what you have left him."

There were other rules which more or less governed the behavior of the deputies. For example, in order not to kill the geese that were laying the golden eggs, a citizen of the town was not to be taxed twice on the same day. That meant that if one of the deputies got to someone before Truitt did, Truitt was out of luck.

Lowman, of course, didn't have to tax anyone directly. In addition to his "liquor tax," he also got a business tax from each of the merchants. Although he shared a portion of his liquor and business taxes with his number one and number two deputies, Bucky and Colby, he kept the lion's share for himself. He was well on his way to becoming a wealthy man without any fear of running afoul of the law.

Truitt was sitting on a chair on the sidewalk in front of Chin Ho's Laundry. From behind him, he could hear the singsong chatter of Chinese at work and smell the sharp odor of strong lye soap. Chin Ho, like the other business owners of the town, was exempt from the personal tax. The business tax he and the others paid to Lowman took care of that. Otherwise, Truitt would have already raised some money from Chin Ho, George Barnet, or Clem Laroche, the barber, for all three had walked by Truitt's vantage point since he'd taken his seat earlier this morning.

Truitt had his chair tipped up against the rip-sawed boards which made up the false front of the laundry. His feet were wrapped around the front legs of the chair and his hat was pulled down low over his eyes. By now the sun was almost dead overhead, so that there were no shadows on the street. This was the hottest time of the day, which meant that most of the town's citizens would stay out of the sun as much as they could. The other deputies were back in the saloon drinking beer and playing cards.

Truitt heard the hollow, clumping sounds of a single rider, and he looked toward the east to see a horseman coming into town. He smiled. If this man was just coming into town, then it was a cinch he hadn't been taxed yet. This one belonged to him.

Truitt tipped his chair forward, then stood up and watched as the rider came into town. Just across the street from the Chinese laundry, the rider pulled up then dismounted in front of the Model Barbershop. As he was tying his horse off at the hitching rail, he was met by Clem Laroche, the barber.

"Yes, sir?" Laroche asked, standing out on the boardwalk in front of his shop. "Would you be wanting a haircut and a shave?"

"Yes," the rider grunted.

"That'll be two bits," the barber answered.

The rider flipped the barber a quarter, then went into the barbershop and took his seat in the single chair. Truitt stayed where he was for a moment, watching as the barber stretched out the chair, then wrapped hot towels around the customer's face. That was when he decided to go over and talk to the stranger.

"Howdy," Truitt said as he stepped inside the barbershop.

The man, whose face was wrapped in towels except for his eyes, opened one eye.

"Howdy," he replied.

"Do you see this here, star?" Truitt asked, pointing to the badge on his vest. By now, Lowman had appointed so many deputies that he had run out of official stars. As a result, the one on Truitt's chest was a crude affair, fashioned from tin by the local blacksmith.

"Not much of a star," the customer grunted.

"Yeah? Well, don't let the looks of it fool you none," Truitt replied. "Cause I'm just as much a deputy as anyone else."

"Well, if that's what you want to be, I'm proud for you," the customer said.

Truitt stroked his chin. This conversation wasn't going exactly as he had planned.

"You ain't gettin' my meanin', mister," Truitt said. "What I'm gettin' at is, as a deputy, I'm duly empowered to collect a tax. So, I reckon I'll just be collectin' from you. It's goin' to cost you two dollars to live here."

"I don't aim to live here," the man in the chair replied. "I'm just passin' through."

"It don't matter none whether you plan to live here or not," Truitt said. "As long as you are here, you are enjoyin' the protection of the sheriff and all his deputies. Now, don't you think that's somethin' worth payin' for?"

"Not particularly."

"Mister," Truitt said in a gruffer voice. "I don't seem to be getting' through to you, do I? I'm here to collect a tax!"

"If it's all the same to you, I guess I'll just pass on the tax and the protection."

Truitt drew his gun. "Now, I can't let you do that," he said. "You see, if I let you get away with not payin' your taxes, why then, the others might think they can try the same thing. Now, you can make it easy on yourself. You can fork over that two dollars like I told you, or..." He let the sentence hang.

"Or what?"

"Or I reckon I could just sift some lead through you, and take ever'thing you got," Truitt said.

"You plannin' on killin' me for two dollars?"

"It ain't the money, it's the principle of the thing," Truitt said. "I wouldn't be killin' you for two dollars. I'd be killin' you just to show ever'one else that you can't get away with not payin' up when you're told." He cocked the pistol and pointed it at the customer's head. "Now, what's it goin' to be, mister? Two dollars or a hole in your head?"

The little barbershop was suddenly filled with the sound of an exploding cartridge. The apron that had been spread over the customer puffed up as a bullet tore through it...from the inside out. The shot left a tiny, brown ring of fire which blazed for an instant, then went out.

After passing through the apron, the bullet hit Truitt in the chest, tore through his heart, then exited just above his left shoulder blade, leaving a quarter-sized wound. The impact propelled Truitt through the door of the barbershop with such force that the door was torn from its hinges. Though he was already dead, the reflex action of his trigger finger caused his own pistol to discharge, firing harmlessly into the board sidewalk in front of the shop. Truitt fell back, face up, off the edge of the sidewalk, landing with his head down in the dirt and his legs still up on the sidewalk itself. A spreading stain of blood soaked the front of his shirt.

The customer stood up from the barber chair and pulled off the punctured apron, then unwrapped the towel from around his face. He stepped outside to look down at Truitt's body. When he saw that Truitt was dead, he went back into the barbershop and retook his place in the chair.

The sound of the gunshot brought several people to the barbershop. The first ones to arrive were the merely curious...shopkeepers and citizens. Amazingly, none of those who came were wearing badges. Apparently, not even a gunshot could get the deputies out into the heat of midday.

One of the citizens who came hurrying toward the sprawled body was Doc Frazer. As he got close enough to see who it was, however, he slowed his pace. By the time he got there, he was at a leisurely walk. Without even bending over, he kicked at the sole of Truitt's boot.

"What about it, Doc?" someone asked.

"This one, I don't mind pronouncin' dead," Doc Frazer replied, and there was a nervous ripple of laughter from the others.

"Who did this?" Doc asked the barber.

"He did," the barber said, pointing with shaking hands to the customer inside.

"Mister," Doc called. "Don't know why the sheriff or none of his deputies showed up to see what the shooting was about, but if you got any sense, you'll ride on now, while you have the chance. With our gratitude," he added.

"Yeah," several other voices agreed.

The customer, who had put the towel around his face a second time, now stood up and removed the towel again. "I haven't even gotten my shave yet," he said.

"You!" Doc Frazer gasped.

"Who is it, Doc?" someone asked quietly.

"It's the fella we were talkin' about," Doc said. "It's Dane Calder."

"Yesterday, you were tryin' to get me to come over. Today, you're tryin' to run me off," Dane said.

"No, sir," Doc Frazer said. "We're not tryin' to run you off. Not by a long shot. You're welcome to stay as long as you want."

"Not only that, you've got the run of the town," Littlefield put in.

Dane looked at Littlefield. "Seems to me like that's how you folks got into trouble in the first place," he said. He sat back down in the barber chair. "I don't want you to get the wrong idea. I'm not takin' your offer. The only thing I want right now is a shave and a haircut."

Dane let Clem Laroche put the apron on him. When the barber saw the brown-ringed hole in the apron and thought again of what had just happened right in front of him, he got nervous. As he raised the razor to Dane's jaw, his hand was shaking visibly. Dane reached up to grab him by the wrist.

"I want my whiskers cut, not my throat," he said.

"Yes, sir," Laroche replied. He took a couple of slow, deep breaths. "I'll be all right now."

"Well, how...how long are you goin' to stay?" Littlefield asked.

"I haven't decided yet," Dane replied. "And I don't want to decide on an empty stomach. Where's the best place to get a meal?"

"The Railroad Café," Laroche said quickly. "Uh, my wife runs it," he said.

"Your wife? Good," Dane said, leaning back in the barber chair. "I reckon I won't have to worry about you cuttin' my throat then. You wouldn't want your wife to lose a customer now, would you?"

Laroche laughed more heartily than the joke called for.

"My wife lose a customer," he said as he began shaving Dane again, his hand somewhat more steady now. "That's a good one. Yes, sir, that's a good one."

TEN

JESSE LOWMAN WAS IN BED WITH ONE OF THE
whores in his room upstairs and at the rear of the
Silver Strike Saloon. He was just at that critical point
when he heard someone pounding on his door.

"Jesse! Jesse, you done in there? Jesse, open up!"

Lowman recognized Bucky's voice. The interrup-
tion caused him to lose his concentration and he fell
to one side of the girl, breathing hard in anger and
frustration.

"I don't know what all the poundin' on that door's
about, Bucky," Lowman yelled, "but it'd better be
good. It'd better be damn good."

"Felix Truitt just got hisself kilt!" Bucky said.

Lowman swung his legs over the side of the bed,
then looked over at the girl. With a modest smile, she
pulled the sheet up to cover her breasts. Though the
heavy green shade was pulled all the way down on his
window, enough of the outside light slipped in around
the edges so that the room was in shadows, giving the

illusion, if not the reality, of coolness. With a sigh, Lowman ran his hand through his tousled hair, then walked over to open the door. Bucky started to come in, but Lowman held him out in the hallway and talked through the crack in the barely opened door.

"Now, what's this about Truitt getting' hisself kilt?" Lowman asked.

"It's just like I said," Bucky replied. "Seems Truitt braced one of the town's citizens to collect some personal tax and the citizen killed him."

"Who did it?"

"I don't know," Bucky admitted. "And to tell you the truth, I don't really much care. I just told you 'cause I figured you'd want to know. But I can't see goin' and makin' no big deal over it. Hell, ole Truitt wan't worth a pound o' dirt in the first place. Good riddance is what I say."

"That ain't the point," Lowman growled. "If one of the good citizens of this town can kill Truitt and get away with it, then someone else might figure they can kill Fontaine, then Wooten, then Colby, then maybe even you, Bucky. And after you, why, they might even want to kill me. You ever looked at it like that?"

"No, I reckon not," Bucky admitted.

"Yeah, well, that's why I'm the sheriff and you're the deputy. All right, never mind. Somethin' like that happens. Folks can't keep quiet about it too long. We'll find out soon enough who it was. You just get on back to your card game and let me be."

"All right, Jesse," Bucky said. He started back, then turned around. "Oh, and I'm sorry 'bout interruptin' you like I done. Did you get finished?"

"That ain't none of your damned business," Lowman growled, slamming the door.

He turned back to the girl, who was still patiently waiting, naked, on the bed. He tried to take up where he left off and the girl was willing, but he was unable to perform. Finally, in a frustrated rage, he pushed the girl out of his bed.

"Get up!" he said angrily. "Get up and get out of here!"

"I'm sorry, honey," the girl said.

"Sorry? You should be sorry, you worthless...."

The girl reached for her clothes and started to get dressed.

"Get out!" Lowman said.

"I just want to get dressed," the girl complained.

"Get dressed somewhere else," Lowman growled. "I don't want to look at your ugly face no more." He opened the door and shoved her, naked and protesting, out into the hall. When she saw Colby walking down the hall, she let out a little shout and made a desperate attempt to cover herself as she ran toward her own room.

"Hell, Clara, it ain't like I ain't seen you before," Lowman heard Colby call. "You was sharin' my bed just two nights ago." Colby laughed as he clumped down the stairs.

Lowman got dressed, then went downstairs to have a little lunch. He saw Colby sitting in his accustomed spot at the table next to the one where Lowman always sat. More and more now, Colby was beginning to get on his nerves, and he wished he had never agreed to take him on as a deputy.

"I seen you throwin' Clara out of your room," Colby said. "What's wrong? Things didn't go too good for you?"

"What are you talkin' about?"

"Most of the time, when a man has a good time with a woman, he treats her a little better than to just throw her out like that." Colby chuckled. "Hell, you didn't even give her time to put on her clothes."

"Colby, you talk too damn much," Lowman said.

* * *

DANE CALDER HAD TAKEN the barber's advice as to where to get a good meal so that, at the same time Lowman was eating at the Silver Strike Saloon, Dane was having lunch at the Railroad Café. The news of Dane's encounter with Felix Truitt had preceded him to the café. As a result, people tended to give him a wide berth, stepping out of his way or purposely taking a table as distant from his as they could. That was fine with Dane, who had always been pretty much of a loner anyway. He ordered ham, eggs, fried potatoes, and coffee from the attractive woman who waited on his table, then ate his meal in silence.

Dane saw a man, woman, and young girl come into the café and take a table. The man was carrying a couple of large carpetbags.

"What if the train comes while we're in here, Papa?" the little girl asked. "If it comes while we're eatin', why, we'll miss it, and then we won't get to see Auntie Em."

"We have a whole hour yet," the girl's father replied. "That's plenty of time for us to eat."

"Are you going on a trip, Mr. Morgan?" one of the other customers asked.

"It's more than a trip, Jeb," Morgan replied. "We're movin' back to Missouri."

"You mean to say you're leavin' Rebel Ridge?" Jeb asked. "But no, Ben, why? You own the only hardware store in town. Folks need you."

"I don't own a hardware store," Morgan growled. "What I own is a supply depot where the sheriff and his deputies can get anything they want, anytime they want, without paying anything close to what it's worth. Besides which, they've scared away all the legitimate customers. No, the question isn't why am I goin'. The question is why anyone else is stayin'. All the merchants are goin' through the same thing."

"But most folks are stickin' it out, Ben. It can't be like this forever."

"It ain't just the stealin'," Mrs. Morgan put in. "It's the killin' too. Why, I heard there was another killin' just this mornin'."

"Yes'm, there was," Jeb said. "Felix Truitt got himself killed. You recall him, don't you, Ben? He's the one who killed Parson Jorgenson. It's good riddance, I say."

"Yes, I know who Truitt is," Morgan replied. "And I agree with you, it's good riddance."

"It would have been even better if they had killed each other," Mrs. Morgan added.

Jeb, who knew that Dane was listening to every

word, cleared his throat and glanced toward Dane's table.

"But I suppose it doesn't really matter," Mrs. Morgan continued, not understanding Jeb's signal. "Whoever killed Truitt today will probably get himself killed tomorrow. You reap what you sow, they say, and the proof was never more in the pudding than the fact that the man who killed our parson just got himself killed."

Jeb cleared his throat again, more loudly this time than before, then glanced pointedly at Dane's table. By now Ben Morgan realized what Jeb was doing, when he, too, looked over toward the table, he recognized Dane from the description he had heard this morning from those who were telling the tale of the great barbershop shootout.

"That's enough, Stella," he said, putting his hand on his wife's arm.

"Well, you know I'm right, Ben Morgan," Stella replied.

"I said that's enough, woman," Ben growled again.

"What your husband is tryin' to tell you, ma'am, is that I'm the one who killed Truitt," Dane said, getting up from his meal. He smiled disarmingly. "But you are quite correct when you say, 'You reap what you sow.' Nobody knows that better than someone in my profession."

With a slight nod, Dane left the café, followed by the wide eyes of every patron in the place.

"What does he mean 'in his profession'?" Dane overheard Mrs. Morgan ask. "What is his profession?"

"He's a bounty hunter, Mrs. Morgan," Jeb answered.

It was always that way with Dane. Anytime he found himself in establishments of normal commerce, such as restaurants, mercantile stores, or railroad and stage depots, he would be around ordinary people. And when he was around ordinary people, he was acutely aware of the great gulf that separated him from civilized society. It was that way even though his profession, as brutal as it was, as distasteful to society as it might be, was very necessary. Without Dane Calder and men like him, the thin line of lawmen who attempted to keep peace in the West would have been strained beyond capacity.

Leaving the restaurant, Dane walked down the street toward the Silver Strike Saloon. He was always much more comfortable in saloons than he was anywhere else, because saloons were the great melting pots of society. Here, one might find an affluent businessman having a social drink with friends while next to them the town drunk lay passed out on the floor. Here, too, the law-abiding and the lawless met on common ground. It was only in saloons that Dane did not feel like such an outcast.

The Silver Strike was very busy, with most of the tables filled by drinking customers, though there were card games in session at three of them. Two of the games were penny-ante games, but there was one which was for much larger stakes.

Dane stepped up to the bar.

"Yes, sir?" the bartender asked as he moved toward Dane.

"I was told I could find a man named Lowman in here," Dane said.

Dane was studying the man's face. From the expression in his eyes when he heard Lowman's name, the bartender wasn't someone the sheriff could count on as a friend.

"Yeah, he's in here most of the time," the bartender said. "But he left just after lunch. Don't know where he went."

"Too bad. I was hopin' to see him."

"Yeah, well, I expect he'll be back," the bartender said. "Don't reckon we're lucky enough to have somethin' happen to him out on the trail."

"Are you wantin' somethin' to happen to him?" Dane asked.

"Wouldn't cry none," the bartender replied easily. "No more'n I did this mornin' when Truitt got hisself killed."

"You didn't like Truitt either?"

"Mister, my job ain't to like or to dislike anyone," the bartender said. "My job is to serve beer and whiskey. Now, you want to drink, or you want to stand here and palaver?"

"I'll have a whiskey."

The bartender made no move.

"Whiskey," Dane said again.

"Heard what you said. Didn't see no money," the bartender replied flatly.

Dane slapped a quarter on the bar, and the bartender responded by filling a glass.

"You aimin' to put on one of them tin stars?" the bartender asked.

"Seems like the job to have in this town," Dane replied.

"Yeah, don't it?" the bartender replied.

Dane took a swallow. The whiskey was green and bitter, not the worst he ever had, but not far from it. "What do you put in this stuff?" he asked. "Kerosene?"

"I wouldn't waste kerosene in it," the bartender replied matter-of-factly. He went back to wiping glasses.

"Wait a minute! Wait a minute, hold it right there!" someone shouted from behind Dane. When he turned, he saw that the loud-voiced man was sitting at the table where the high-stakes game was being played. "I had a pair of aces up. How'd you know I didn't have them backed up?"

"I didn't know," a powerfully built man across the table answered. "I was just playing a hunch."

"Like hell you was. You knew what my hole card was."

There was a scrape of chairs as the other players began backing away from the table. Dane watched with cool detachment, noticing that all the participants were wearing the tin stars of deputies.

"You ain't sayin' I'm cheatin' or anythin' like that, are you, Baxter?"

"No, Bucky, it ain't nothin' like that," Baxter replied more cautiously. "I...I was just admirin' your luck in guessin' when to call, is all."

Dane looked over at the man called Bucky. He knew who he was, for he had run across the man's name and description on a few wanted posters. Bucky was a bully who got his way by beating up people.

That trait made him, perhaps, the least liked of all of Lowman's deputies. On the other hand, one who used his fists as often as Bucky was less likely to use his gun. As a result, the crimes Bucky was wanted for weren't enough to cause anyone to put up much reward money, or to even have his likeness put on the dodgers.

Bucky noticed Dane leaning against the bar staring at him, and he looked up. "Want to sit in, mister?" he asked.

Dane set his glass down. "Might do it at that," he replied.

"Come on, then, I reckon your money's as good as anyone's."

Eleven

Dane ambled over to the table and pulled out a chair, then dropped three gold double eagles on the table in front of him.

"You ain't one of the local citizens," Bucky commented. "Are you?"

"Can't say as I am."

As Bucky began to deal, he studied Dane through narrow-slit eyes. "Do I know you?" Bucky asked.

"Don't know if you do or not," Dane replied without elaboration.

"They's somethin' 'bout you that's naggin' at me," he said. He continued to study Dane. "It'll come to me," he said. "It nearly always does."

"I'm sure it will," Dane said easily.

They were playing five-card draw and Dane lost ten dollars on the first hand, folding cautiously with a hand that was better than the hand Bucky was using to run his bluff.

"Ha!" Bucky said, pulling in his winnings. "Maybe I

should'a warned you. When I play this game, I don't give no quarter."

Dane folded his second hand the same way he had his first, and again Bucky, who was the winner, chuckled as he raked in the pot.

When the pot on the third hand reached forty dollars, Dane, who had drawn one card to complete a flush, bet five dollars.

"Better watch yourself there, now," Bucky said. "You go an' try to make it all back in one hand. I'm goin' to clean you out good. Want me to show you what I mean? Here's your five, and I'm raisin' you five."

Easily and confidently, Bucky pushed ten dollars into the pot.

Dane studied his hand carefully and once nearly folded. Then, as if he were very unsure of himself, he called.

"All right, mister, let's see what you were holdin'," Bucky said, putting down his own jack-high straight.

Dane put down his diamond flush.

"Damn, you had that good a hand an' you just sit there holdin' it like that? You should'a raised instead of called," Bucky said. "Ain't you ever played this game before?"

"Sure I've played," Dane said, as if offended by the remark. "I'm doin' all right. I won, didn't I?"

"You won?" Bucky snorted. "Mister, you think you're somethin' because you won one lousy pot?"

Dane looked at the pile of money in front of his position. "I got more money now than I started with," he said. "In my book, that makes me better than you." He had been playing to Bucky's vanity ever since he sat down, and now it was beginning to pay off. He could see Bucky getting piqued at the thought of losing a game to someone as amateurish as he thought Dane was.

"You think you're better'n me, huh?" Bucky said. "You sure enough of yourself to up the ante?"

"I don't know if I should," Dane said. "I mean, not with you dealin' the cards."

"You think I'm cheatin', do you?" Bucky challenged angrily.

Dane chuckled. "Not really," he answered. "I reckon if you was cheatin', you'd be winnin'. Right now, you're losin'. But if I'm goin' to bet more, I want to deal."

The others around the table, all of whom had been losing to Bucky, laughed, now, at Bucky's expense.

Angry, Bucky slid the cards across the table. "All right, Mr. Gamblin' Man. You deal."

"Thanks," Dane replied. He picked up the cards and began feeling them as he shuffled. He checked for pinpricks and uneven corners. There didn't appear to be any, which meant that the deck, at least, was honest.

"Now," Bucky said, eyeing the money in front of Dane. "What do you say we get to the nut-cuttin'? Let's ante twenty dollars."

Dane pushed twenty dollars into the pot, but the ante was enough to run all but one of the other players away.

Dane dealt the cards, and as Bucky picked them up, his smile grew broader. "All right," he said. "I'm goin' to open for another twenty bucks."

The third player who had stayed through the ante now groaned and threw in his cards.

"It's up to you, mister," Bucky said. "You goin' to play or fold?"

"I'll see your twenty," Dane said, sliding the money into the pot. Then he reached into his pocket and pulled out five gold double eagles. "And I'll raise you one hundred."

The easy smile left Bucky's face, and he stared at Dane, shocked not only by the amount of money Dane had bet but also by the ease with which he'd bet it. This was not the timid, bungling cowpoke he thought he had been playing against.

At first, Bucky started to respond to the hundred-dollar bet by raising again. But even as he put his hands on the money, he realized it would be a sucker bet. The stranger had set a trap, and he'd fallen for it.

The others around the table understood what was going on as quickly as Bucky had, and they began to laugh.

"Well now, Bucky, what are you going to do next?" one of them asked.

"Yeah, looks to me like he's drawn you in slick as a whistle," another said.

Bucky put the money down and stared at the pot. They were right. He had been suckered. It would cost him a hundred dollars now just to stay, but he couldn't fold, not with three aces and a chance to improve it with the draw. Slowly, he slid one hundred dollars out into the center of the table.

"All right, mister," he growled. "I'll take two cards.

And you'd better be particular careful with your deal, 'cause I'm gonna be watchin' you awful close."

Dane's eyes narrowed. "Are you suggestin' I'm cheatin' you?" he asked.

"Ain't makin' no suggestion of the kind," Bucky answered. "I'm just tellin' you that I'm goin' to be watchin' pretty close, that's all."

"How many cards?"

"Two," Bucky replied.

Dane dealt two cards and Bucky groaned inwardly, when he picked them up. His three aces weren't improved.

"I'll play with what I have," Dane said. "It's still your bet."

"I'll check to the dealer," Bucky suggested, knowing even as he spoke that his opponent wasn't going to let that stand.

"Not so easy. It's goin' to cost you another one hundred," Dane said easily, sliding five more gold coins into the center of the table.

"Mister, how does a cowpoke like you come by such money?" Bucky asked.

"Where the money came from isn't the question," Dane answered. He nodded toward the center of the table. "The question is, are you goin' to see my bet?"

With an angry snort, Bucky threw in his cards. "Three aces!" he said. "What are the chances of losin' when you're holdin' three aces in a two-handed game?"

Carefully, Dane lay his cards on the table, face-down. Then, smiling, he reached for the pot and pulled it toward him.

"Not all that much, I reckon," he said. "But you just got beat."

"Not yet, I ain't beat," Bucky growled, reaching down to clamp his hand around Dane's wrist. "Let me see what you got."

Dane looked at Bucky coolly. "Mister, you didn't pay to see what I have," he said.

"Like hell I didn't. I put a hundred and forty dollars into this pot, and I say that buys me a look."

Dane held Bucky in his gaze for another moment, then he smiled, though the smile never reached his eyes. "All right," he said. "Here's what beat you."

Dane turned his cards over. He had a pair of nines, a jack of spades, a seven of clubs, and a three of diamonds.

"What the hell?" Bucky sputtered. "Mister, I don't know who you are or what you're tryin' to pull. But I don't plan to just sit here an' let you steal a hand from me."

"Don't look to me like he stole it, Bucky," one of the other players said. "Looks to me like he won it, fair and square. He called your bluff."

"He ain't getting' this hand," Bucky said. "He didn't even have openers."

"I didn't open," Dane reminded him. "You did." Dane reached for the cards, but before he could get them, Bucky sent a roundhouse right across the table, connecting squarely with Dane's jaw and dropping him to the floor.

"Well, then," Bucky growled. "How's that for openers?" He started to reach for the pot, but Dane jumped up, quickly, sending a whistling left punch which landed squarely on Bucky's chin, knocking him away from the table, but not putting him down.

Bucky was a man who lived by brute strength and his strength had just been challenged by someone who was three inches shorter and at least seventy pounds lighter. He smiled at Dane, and Dane was somewhat taken aback. He had hit Bucky hard enough to stun a bull, yet Bucky hadn't gone down.

"So you want to play my game, do you?" Bucky asked, rubbing his chin. He chuckled. "Well, now, ain't that fine? I reckon Christmas has come early for ole Bucky Zorn. Yes, sir, I'm goin' to clean your plow good."

"Mister, you just made yourself one big mistake," one of the other card players said. "Ain't no one ever got the better of Bucky."

Dane, being a man of few words, didn't respond to either comment. Instead, he sent another quick slashing left into Bucky's face. It was a good, well-delivered blow, but Bucky just flinched, then laughed a low, evil laugh.

"Fight! They's a fight in the saloon!" someone shouted across the batwing doors, and within a few seconds there were twice as many people in the saloon as there had been when Dane had thrown his first punch.

Dane and Bucky circled slowly to their left, studying each other over raised fists as the crowd in the saloon increased.

"I've got five bucks on Bucky," someone shouted.

"I got ten on him!"

"I'll take the bets," another said. "I've seen fellas

like this one before, skinny and wiry. You ask me, he's tough as rawhide."

Bucky, perhaps spurred on by the fact that someone would actually consider betting against him, rushed forward like a charging bull. Dane stepped nimbly to one side, and Bucky crashed into the table where they had been playing, smashing it to kindling wood and spilling the money and cards to the floor. With an angry roar, he turned to face Dane a second time.

"Stand still, you chicken-livered bastard!" he shouted.

The crowd continued to urge the two men on, shouting their encouragement to one or the other. Many of them were wearing the badges of authority, yet some of them were rooting for Dane. That was because even they were often bullied by Lowman's chief deputy.

Bucky swung a club-like swing, which Dane easily avoided. Dane counterpunched, and again he scored well. Again, however, Bucky merely laughed it off.

A pattern began to emerge as the fight continued. It was obvious that Dane could hit Bucky at will, though the punches, individually, had no noticeable effect. However, there was a cumulative effect to the punches, as both of Bucky's eyes were beginning to puff up, and there was a nasty cut on his lip. Then Dane caught Bucky in the nose with a long left, and when he felt the nose fold up under his hand, he knew he had broken it. The bridge of Bucky's nose exploded like a smashed tomato and started bleeding profusely. The blood ran across Bucky's teeth and chin.

Dane began to look for another chance at the nose, but Bucky started protecting it. Dane was unable to get to it again, though the fact that Bucky was so protective of it told Dane, at least, that the nose was hurting him.

So far, except for the very first unexpected blow, Bucky had not even connected. The big man was throwing great swinging blows toward Dane, barely missing him, but as yet, Dane was untouched.

After four or five such blows, Dane noticed that Bucky was leaving a slight opening for a good right punch, if he could just slip it in across Bucky's shoulder. He timed it, and on Bucky's next swing, Dane threw a solid right straight at the place where he thought Bucky's nose would be. He hit it perfectly and had the satisfaction of hearing a bellow of pain from Bucky for the first time.

Bucky was obviously growing more tired now, and he began charging more and swinging less. Dane got set for one of his charges; then, as Bucky rushed by with his head down, Dane stepped to one side. Like a matador thrusting his sword into the bull in a killing lunge, Dane sent a powerful right jab to Bucky's jaw. Bucky went down and out.

For a moment the people in the saloon, who had been noisy partisans during the fight, were stunned into silence. Then from the crowd there came the sound of a solitary person clapping his hands. Dane looked toward the bar to see Jesse Lowman standing there, clapping his hands together pointedly.

"Well, well, well," Lowman said. "If it isn't my old pal, Dane Calder."

"Calder!" someone gasped.

"Is this the bounty hunter?" another asked.

"Calder," another said, and the name was repeated in awestruck tones throughout the crowd.

"Hello, Lowman," Dane said as he bent down to pick up his winnings from the floor.

"I got word you weren't goin' to come. I heard you turned down the town's offer."

"I did turn down the offer."

"Then what are you doin' here, in Rebel Ridge?"

"I figure where I go and when I go is nobody's business but my own," Dane said.

He stepped up to the bar, and Newberry handed him a whiskey. When Dane tasted it, it was smooth, much better than the rotgut he had drunk when he first came in. When he looked at the bartender in surprise, the bartender let just the suggestion of a smile play across his lips.

"Normally, I reckon that might be true," Lowman said. "But bein' as I'm the sheriff here, I sort of have a stake in what goes on in my town. Especially if someone is goin' to come into my town and start shootin' and beatin' up all my deputies. That was you shot Truitt this mornin' wasn't it?"

"He never told me his name," Dane said.

Lowman chuckled dryly. "Well, at least you ain't denyin' it."

"Why should I deny it? I had every right to shoot him. He was about to shoot me."

"Yeah, well, Truitt never was very careful 'bout things like that. So, what are you figurin' on doin' now?"

"I haven't thought much about it."

"How'd you like to throw in with me? I can make you a pretty good offer," Lowman suggested.

"I wasn't interested in the town's offer; what makes you think I'd be interested in yours?"

"'Cause I can offer you a lot more. Besides which, you owe me."

Dane looked at Lowman. "I owe you?"

"Sure. I could'a kilt you the last time we met. Only I didn't."

"No. Instead, you left me for the buzzards."

"You're here."

"Yeah, I'm here," Dane said.

"So, like I say, you owe me. Now, how 'bout throwin' in with me. With the two of us workin' together, we can suck this town dry...then go on to another one and start all over again." Bucky who was still on the floor but was now coming around, laughed. "Hell, it's better'n robbin' a bank," Lowman added.

"How would you know? You've never robbed a bank."

"What makes you think I haven't?"

Dane finished his drink, then wiped his mouth with the back of his hand.

"Because if you had, there would be a big enough reward on you to make it worth my comin' after you," Dane answered. "The way it is now neither you"— Dane looked around at the other deputies, all of whom were now following the conversation from a safe distance—"nor any of these other saddle tramps you have around you are worth a bucket of dirt."

Dane put his glass down on the bar and started

toward the batwing doors. Lowman, watching him leave, grew tempted by the target of Dane's back. Slowly and unobtrusively, he started to move his right hand toward his pistol.

Even though his back was turned, Dane, somehow, sensed Lowman's movement. Dane stopped. All he did was stop...but that was enough for Lowman. Slowly, Lowman let his gun hand drop back down by his side.

Without turning or saying a word, Dane walked out of the saloon.

TWELVE

DANE TOOK A ROOM IN THE COMMERCIAL HOTEL. He had a bath, then a good dinner in the hotel dining room. Several people noticed him during dinner, and he saw that they were talking about him, but no one came over to talk to him. After dinner, Dane bought a cigar from the hotel tobacconist, then walked outside to take another look at the town.

It was after eight o'clock now, and the sun was a bright red orb, low in the western sky. The fading light was kind to the town so that the buildings, which had looked bleak and harsh in the noonday sun, were now rimmed with gold and flushed with crimson. A young paperboy carrying a bundle of one-page news sheets passed by, hawking his product.

"Paper, mister? Get your paper?"

Dane gave the boy a penny and took one of the papers. "FELIX TRUITT KILLED IN SHOOTOUT ON MAIN STREET," the headline read over one of the stories. Dane read on.

Yet another shooting has taken place on the streets of what was once an industrious and productive town. Felix Truitt, one of the many deputies illegally appointed by Sheriff Jesse Lowman, was shot down in front of the barbershop today by a man identified as Dane Calder.

According to an eyewitness who does not wish to be identified, Dane Calder came into his shop for a haircut and was accosted by Truitt shortly after taking his seat in the barber chair.

"I'll be collecting the tax from you," Truitt is reported to have said.

"What tax would that be?" Mr. Calder replied.

"Why, the personal tax, of course," Truitt explained, speaking of that accursed tax which has placed such an unfair burden upon all the good citizens of this beleaguered city.

"Sir, I am but a stranger in your midst and know nothing of this tax," Mr. Calder responded.

"Stranger or not, you must pay the tax," Truitt ordered.

"I have no wish to participate," Mr. Calder answered.

Upon hearing such an answer, Truitt pulled his pistol and held it within inches of Mr. Calder's face. "You shall pay the tax," Truitt ordered, "or I shall sift some lead through you."

Mr. Calder is said to have made no reply, nor to have taken any action, until such time as he saw Truitt cock the hammer on the pistol he was holding, a fair indication, if one be needed, that the .44-caliber engine of death was about to be used. Whereupon, our unnamed eyewitness reports, the interior of his tonsorial establishment was filled with the noise of exploding gunpowder. The ball thus energized, however, did not come from Felix Truitt's .44, but from

Dane Calder's pistol, the weapon having been discharged from beneath the barber's apron which had been placed upon Mr. Calder's person in preparation for a shave and haircut.

While the death of any human being is a somber event, there are, nevertheless, times when such an occasion is necessary. Legal hangings of desperadoes are one such example. The death of Felix Truitt is another, for while not singly responsible for, he was, nevertheless, representative of all that is wrong with our fair town. This writer feels reasonably certain in making the statement that there are none who will mourn his passing.

While it may have been a bullet fired from Dane Calder's pistol which dispatched Felix Truitt to his appointed rendezvous with the devil himself, in doing so, Dane Calder was but the instrument of justice.

Dane was pleased to see that not everyone in the town of Rebel Ridge was content to let Lowman and his deputies run roughshod over them. At least the newspaper editor seemed to have gumption enough to speak out.

Over in the Silver Strike Saloon, however, the reaction to the newspaper article wasn't as positive. Fontaine read the story to Wooten, Jacobs, and Colby. Afterward, he laid the paper down.

"Well, what do you think of that?" he asked. "This newspaper fella all but said Truitt got what was comin' to him."

"Yeah, well, you got to give it to the little sonofabitch for guts," Wooten said.

"And where do you think he got the guts to print

somethin' like that? You think he would'a printed this last week? Hell, you think he would'a done it yesterday?"

"Prob'ly not," Wooten agreed.

"What you getting' at, anyway, Fontaine?" Jacobs asked.

"I'm thinkin' we're gonna have to do somethin', and we're gonna have to do it quick," Fontaine said. "That's my friend lyin' dead up there in Parker's Undertaking Parlor. Calder kilt him in cold blood, an' they ain't none of us doin' nothin' about it."

"Truth to tell, I ain't cryin' much over Truitt. He was your friend, he wasn't mine," Colby said.

"Yeah," Jacobs agreed. "You want to do somethin' about it, do it yourself."

"I can't handle Calder all by myself," Fontaine admitted. "I don't know, Colby, maybe you can."

"If I go up against Calder, it's goin' to have to be for some reason better'n getting' even for Truitt," Colby said.

"Yeah, well, how's this for a reason? Lowman wants to get Calder to join in with us."

"Well, hell, what's wrong with that?" Wooten asked.

"What's wrong with that? I'll tell you what's wrong with that. If Calder comes in with Lowman, he'll come in at the top. You know what that does to the rest of us? That'll move us all down one notch. Colby, you'll be pickin' among the chickens with the rest of us, trying to shake down the citizens for personal tax. That'll be less for you...and less for us."

"Uh-uh," Colby said. "Ain't no way I'm goin' to get out there with you fellas, chasin' down the citizens."

"Then we're goin' to have to do somethin' about Dane Calder," Fontaine insisted.

"If it goes that far, then I'll worry about it," Colby said. "In the meantime, leave me out of it."

"Somebody's got to do somethin'," Fontaine insisted.

"What can we do?" Wooten asked. "Especially if we don't have Colby on our side. Nothin', that's what."

"Maybe we can't do nothin' about Calder yet," Fontaine agreed. "But I don't figure to just stand by an' let the rest of the town get ideas from some snot-nosed newspaper man. I think we should pay him a little visit."

"And do what?" Jacobs asked.

Fontaine smiled evilly. "Why, congratulate him on his fine article," he said.

Wooten chuckled. "Yeah," he said. "Yeah, I think that might be a good idea."

"Me too," Jacobs threw in.

"How 'bout you, Colby? You with us?" Bodine asked.

Colby shook his head. "Like I told you, Truitt wasn't nothin' to me. You want to do somethin' to the newspaper man, you go right ahead. I got better things to do."

"All right, we'll take care of it ourselves," Fontaine said. He laughed. "How hard can it be, anyway? He's just one skinny little newspaperman."

Emboldened by one more drink, the three deputies

left the saloon and walked down the street to the office of the *Rebel Ridge Vindicator*.

A smallish, balding man wearing an ink-stained apron looked up from a platen where he was busy setting type. "Can I help you gentlemen?" he asked.

"You the fella that wrote this here story?" Fontaine asked, holding up the single-sheet paper.

"Brandon L. Pipkin, that's me," the newspaperman replied.

"We don't much like what you said," Fontaine growled.

Pipkin chuckled. "That's good," he said.

"Good? What do you mean, good?"

"A newspaper that elicits no response from its readers is not doing its job. The fact that you have a response means that my newspaper is an effective organ of the people. Now, do you wish to register a complaint?"

Fontaine smiled. "Yeah," he said. "Yeah, a complaint. That's what we want to do."

"Excellent, excellent. Suppose I get you a piece of paper and a pencil? You can sit down right over there and write a letter. I'll print it in the next issue and we can get a real dialogue going."

"Letter? What are you talkin' about? I ain't here to write you no letter."

"I'm afraid I don't understand," Pipkin said. "I thought you said you were here to register a complaint."

"Yeah," Fontaine replied. He grinned evilly. "This kind of complaint."

Fontaine pushed over the printing press, then

picked up one of the type boxes and threw it through the window.

"Hey! What...what are you doing?" Pipkin shouted. "Stop that!"

"Stop that!" Fontaine mimicked in a high-pitched, singsong voice. He picked up another box of type and threw it through the space where the window had been. This box, like the first, landed in the street, spilling its type into the dirt. Wooten and Jacobs also got into the action so that, soon, the street in front of the newspaper office was littered with type, paper, ink brushes, and other tools of the newspaper trade.

Pipkin ran out into the street and began making a desperate effort to recover his property. By now several other citizens of the town had been drawn to the scene, and they stood around in nervous, uncomfortable silence, watching Pipkin crawl through the dirt.

"Help me, somebody," Pipkin pleaded. "Won't somebody help me?"

Littlefield kneeled down beside Pipkin and began helping him pick up the scattered type.

"What is the meaning of all this?" he asked.

"Leave it on the ground," Fontaine demanded.

"What?"

Fontaine drew his pistol and pulled the hammer back. "I said, leave it on the ground," he repeated. "Unless you're aimin' to buy into some of this fella's trouble."

Littlefield looked at all the others who had gathered around, imploring them by the expression on his face to join him in this protest. No one responded. Instead, they all looked at the ground, sheepishly.

* * *

DANE CALDER HAD BEEN at the far end of the street when he heard the crashing of the window glass. He was just arriving as Littlefield stood up, dusting his hands together. Seeing Dane, Littlefield smiled.

"Mr. Calder, you'll help, won't you?" he asked.

Dane saw Fontaine standing there with his pistol already drawn.

"You plannin' on mixin' in this, Calder?" Fontaine asked menacingly.

Dane shook his head. "Nope," he replied. "This is none of my business."

"Mr. Calder, please!" the newspaperman cried. "Surely you have some appreciation for freedom of the press?"

"The press wasn't free this evenin'," Dane replied easily. "It cost me a penny."

The others laughed nervously.

"Yeah," Fontaine said. "Can you imagine chargin' a penny for that? I think you ought to give ever'one their money back. And you can start with Mr. Calder here."

Dane held up his hand. "I don't want my money back," he said. "I thought it was well worth the penny. It was a good story."

"Well, now, wait a minute here," Wooten said. "Are you for us or against us?"

"I'm not either one," Dane replied. "Like I said, this is none of my business."

"The way I heard it," Fontaine said, "the sheriff was plannin' on fixin' it so's it *was* your business. You are joinin' up with us, aren't you?"

"I have no such plans," Dane said. He started to walk away.

"Is that a fact? Jesse is goin' to be real disappointed to hear that," Fontaine said. "He's figurin' on you joinin' us. And the way I look at it, you're either for us, or against us. Now which is it?"

"I'm damn sure not for you," Dane replied. Again, he started to walk away.

"Hold on there, mister," Fontaine said. "I don't like the way you keep walkin' away from a friendly discussion."

Dane sighed, then turned around. He had made every effort to avoid this, but it was too late now. There was only one way to settle the issue.

"What is your name, mister?"

"The name is Fontaine. William T. Fontaine. Me and Felix Truitt was real good friends. Truitt is the name of the man you kilt."

"You're not very careful about choosin' your friends, are you?"

"I heard you shot him through the barber apron. Is that true?"

"I reckon it is."

"I call that a dirty way to kill a man."

"Killin' isn't clean, no matter how you do it," Dane replied.

"Truitt never had a chance."

Dane shook his head. "That's right," he said.

"You...you admit it!" Fontaine sputtered.

"That's right," Dane said. "I admit it. Now, you say your name is Fontaine, is it?"

"Yeah."

"Fontaine, I want you to help the newspaper editor here pick up his type."

There was a collective gasp of surprise from the onlookers.

Fontaine let out a short, ugly laugh.

"You gone loco, Calder? Tellin' me to help pick up this type?"

"You tell 'im, Fontaine," Wooten said.

"No, don't tell 'im nothin'. Just gut-shoot the sonofabitch right there where he's a'standin'," Jacobs put in.

"I don't plan to tell you again," Dane said. His words were soft and cajoling, rather than loud and demanding. And yet, it was that cold, emotionless softness that made the words frightening. "Pick up the newspaper man's type."

"Calder, you got more nerve and less sense than anyone I ever seen," Fontaine said. He moved the pistol so that it was pointing toward Dane. "Don't you see I got the drop on you? All I got to do is pull the trigger."

Dane shook his head slowly. "No," he said. "You may try to pull the trigger, but I'll kill you before you can get the job done."

Fontaine laughed a nervous little laugh that was as dry as the rattle of bare tree limbs in a hot desert wind. "You'll do what? You may not have noticed it, Calder, but your gun is still in your holster. I could kill you now and no one would fault me for it. In fact, I'd be a hero." He giggled. "I'd be doin' what Lowman and Colby are afraid to do."

"Pick up the type, Fontaine, or die with the gun in your hand," Dane said.

The crowd, which had originally been drawn to a noisy altercation, now stood transfixed by the scene that was playing out before them. Like Fontaine, they had heard Dane Calder threaten to kill him if he didn't help the newspaperman pick up his type. And like Fontaine, they wondered if, perhaps, Dane Calder had lost his senses, for Fontaine clearly had the drop on Dane.

"Shoot 'im, Fontaine, shoot 'im," Wooten said anxiously.

"Yeah, shoot the sonofabitch!" Jacobs added. Though they could no more understand how Fontaine might be in danger than could Fontaine himself, and they couldn't hold back the cold bile of fear that was beginning to well up in each of them.

Fontaine forced himself to smile, then started to thumb back the hammer on his pistol. He didn't even get it half-cocked before Dane had his own gun in his hand. There was a snap of primer cap, then a roar of exploding powder, though both events happened so quickly as to be one loud bang. A finger of flame shot from the end of Dane's pistol. Fontaine dropped his gun and grabbed his chest. His eyes opened wide in pain and shock. He fell against the doorjamb of the newspaper office, then slid down to the sidewalk, leaving a smear of blood on the wall behind him. He wound up in a sitting position, his eyes open and blank.

"My god, did you see that?" someone in the crowd asked. "Calder just kilt Fontaine while Fontaine was holdin' a gun in his hand the whole time."

"I ain't never seen anyone that fast."

Dane looked at the other two deputies. Neither of them had drawn, having felt secure in the fact that Fontaine already had his pistol out and in the firing position.

Shooting Fontaine had been easy, but only someone with Dane's experience would realize that. Dane had looked deep into Fontaine's eyes and knew he would stop and think before he actually pulled the trigger. And, while Fontaine was thinking about it, Dane was already doing it. Drawing and shooting for someone with Dane's speed, was one step...not two.

"How about you two fellas helpin' the newspaper man here pick up the type?" Dane ordered.

"Yes, sir," Wooten mumbled.

"No! Get away from me! All of you!" the newspaperman shouted. "I'll pick up my own damn type!"

Dane looked at the newspaperman for a moment, then put his gun in his holster. As he walked away, he could feel the two deputies' eyes boring holes in his neck. He knew they were too afraid to draw.

THIRTEEN

THERE WERE SEVERAL PEOPLE GATHERED ON THE street in front of Morgan's Hardware, even though the store was closed now that Ben Morgan and his family had taken the train back to Missouri. However, Parker's Undertaking Parlor, which was attached to the rear of the building, was still in business, and it was this fact that had drawn the crowd. Littlefield had to pick his way through them in order to go down the side alley to the back entrance of the mortuary.

"Are you goin' inside the funeral parlor, Mr. Littlefield?" someone asked.

"Yes, I am."

"Ask 'em how much longer it will be."

"How much longer what will be?" Littlefield asked.

"How much longer will it be until they bring the bodies up here and put 'em on display? I hear Sheriff Lowman is goin' to have them laid out in the window of Morgan's Hardware."

"Yes, that's what I heard, too," Littlefield said.

"So, find out how much longer, will you?"

"I have no intention of satisfyin' your ghoulish curiosity," Littlefield growled. "Now, if you will excuse me?"

Once inside the funeral parlor, Littlefield saw Doc Frazer and George Barnet talking to Gus Parker. Parker was dressed all in black, as was his custom, and he was wearing a stovepipe hat. Behind him, Littlefield could see Fontaine's body. It was naked, and Littlefield could see the neat black hole just to the left of center in his chest. On another table lay Truitt's body. Truitt was already dressed in his burial suit. It was dark, with a stiff, white shirtfront and a gray silk bowtie.

"Gus, you aren't really goin' to display those corpses in the window, are you?" Littlefield asked.

"Yes, I am," Parker answered.

"But that's macabre! Why would you do such a thing?"

"Because I ain't got no choice in the matter. Sheriff Lowman has ordered it done," Parker said. He pointed to two black lacquered coffins ornately decorated with silver trim. "And he has chosen two of my finest coffins."

"Did he pay you for them?" Barnet asked.

"I reckon you could say that...if you figure ten dollars apiece pays for 'em."

"They look more expensive than that."

"Ten dollars is about ten percent of what they are actually worth," Gus replied. He smiled. "I'll tell you this though. These two august gentlemen may be displayed in these coffins but they'll never be buried in them. When they go in the ground, they'll be in plain pine boxes."

"Jarred, did you see the sign the sheriff wants to put in the window?" Barnet asked, showing Littlefield a hand-lettered sign:

KILLED IN THE STREETS OF REBEL RIDGE

BY THE BOUNTY HUNTER DANE CALDER

TWO FINE DEPUTIES

FELIX TRUITT

WILLIAM T. FONTAINE

LITTLEFIELD SIGHED, then handed the sign back to Barnet. "I have a feelin' there are goin' to be more."

"Yes, well, as long as it is men like these two, you'll get no complaint from me," Barnet said.

"Yes, but it may not be men like these. The next person to die may be an innocent citizen."

"Maybe we made a mistake in contacting Calder," Parker suggested. "You never should have gone over there to see him, Doc."

"Now, hold on a minute there, Gus," Doc Frazer said. "This wasn't my idea. In fact, I was opposed to it. But I seem to recall a donation from you, quick enough, right after the parson got killed."

"I wasn't the only one," Parker insisted.

"Anyway, you might have been against it to begin with, but you was the one who went to him with the offer," Barnet said.

"So what if I did? He didn't accept our offer," Frazer pointed out.

"Which, in my mind, makes it all the worse," Barnet replied.

"How do you figure that?" Parker asked.

"Well, if he was workin' for us, we could call him off now, tell him we don't want him over here anymore. But, bein' as he's here on his own, we got no say in the matter. No say at all."

"At least he's on our side," Littlefield suggested.

Barnet shook his head. "I wish I could believe that," he said. "But if you ask me, he ain't on nobody's side but his own. You were over at the newspaper office, Jarred, you saw what happened. Why, Calder wasn't even goin' to help Pipkin at all, until Fontaine made him mad. What if it had been some citizen who made him mad? Or you? You were there. Suppose Calder had decided to take his wrath out on you? It would be you lyin' naked over there on that table, waitin' for Gus to put the formaldehyde into you."

"What are you suggestin', George? That we now ask Calder to leave, the way we asked him to come?"

"It's worth a try."

"No," Doc said. "We'll do no such thing."

"Doc, I figured you'd be the first one to go along with the idea," Barnet said. "Seein' as you didn't want him here in the first place."

"You fellas don't know Calder."

"And you do?"

"I think so," Doc said.

"When did you get to be such close friends?"

"I didn't say we were friends. I just said I know him...or at least, I know the measure of the man," he added. "Don't forget, he turned down our offer, because he was able to draw the line between bounty huntin' and killin' for hire. I'm not really sure why he is here, now. But I sincerely believe that no one who is innocent has anything to fear from him. I say we just stay out of it. Things have been set in motion now... let's let it run its course."

"I agree," Littlefield said. "George?"

George nodded. "All right," he said. "I'll go along." He chuckled. "I guess there's really not much else we can do."

* * *

WHEN DANE WALKED by the hardware store a little later, he saw a crowd gathered around the front window. Curious, he went over to see what held their attention. When they saw him coming, they parted like the sea before Moses so that Dane could have an unrestricted view of the ghoulish display of the two corpses.

KILLED IN THE STREETS OF REBEL RIDGE

BY THE BOUNTY HUNTER DANE CALDER

TWO FINE DEPUTIES

FELIX TRUITT

WILLIAM T. FONTAINE

The bodies of Truitt and Fontaine lay side by side. They were, as Lowman had ordered, lying in shiny black coffins which were decorated with ornate silver trim. The hinges were of silver, and at the foot of each coffin there was a spray of silver oak leaves. Just under the viewing glass was a large, spread-winged silver eagle, and right above the eagle, a silver plate with the name of the deceased inscribed.

The head and shoulders of each of the men were visible through the viewing glass. Felix Truitt looked as peaceful as if he were sleeping. Fontaine, however, wore a vivid mast of death. His eyes had crept half-open and his upper lip was pulled up, showing his teeth. The edge of his mouth and his cheeks were set in a grimace as if he were fighting against the pain of the bullet which had struck him.

"Excuse me, Mr. Calder," someone said. "But would you mind standin' just to the left of the window there so I could get you in this here picture?"

The man who asked the question was setting up a tall, tripod-mounted camera. He draped a black cloth over the camera, then got under it to view the scene through his lens.

"And if you would, hold a pistol across your chest, thus," the photographer said. "Oh," he said in a sudden burst of enthusiasm. "Do you know what would really look good? If you had two pistols instead of one and if you crossed your arms across your chest like this." The photographer demonstrated.

"Get someone else for your picture," Dane grunted. He started down the street toward the newspaper office.

* * *

BRANDON L. PIPKIN had managed to get the press back upright and was now tightening the components that had been loosened when it was pushed over. When he heard someone come through the front door, he grabbed a crowbar, then stood up and turned around, prepared, if need be, to do battle.

"Take it easy," Dane said, holding out his hands. "I'm not your enemy,"

Pipkin lowered the crowbar. "No," he said. "I suppose you aren't."

Dane chuckled. "Were you really goin' to hit me with that thing?"

"If you were bent upon doing further damage to my equipment, the answer is an unequivocal yes," Pipkin responded. He laid the crowbar down, then got back onto his knees and picked up a screwdriver.

"You havin' troubles with it?"

"The tympanum was dislodged," Pipkin said, tightening the hinged wooden cover.

"From the way those men went through here, I'm surprised there isn't more damage," Dane replied.

"Yes. Well, the Washington hand press is, perhaps, the sturdiest press ever built," Pipkin bragged. "However, even it can be damaged if one sets out to do so."

Finishing his adjustments, Pipkin stood up, moved the tympanum over the bed, then raised it up a dozen times to test it. Satisfied, he wiped his hands on his apron, then looked at Dane.

"Please forgive me for what might seem to you a lack of appreciation," he said. "I am grateful that your intervention prevented any further damage to myself or my shop. However, the way you did it, by killing Fontaine, is the antithesis of all that I stand for."

Dane chuckled. "You do use big words," he said. "What does 'antithesis' mean?"

"It means 'just the opposite,'" Pipkin explained. "Have you ever heard the expression 'throwing out the baby with the bathwater'?"

"Yes."

Pipkin scratched his cheek, and in doing so, left a small ink stain. "That's what I see happening to Rebel Ridge," he said. "You see, we are controlled by evil men with violent ways. You, Mr. Calder, have a less evil intent...but your ways are just as violent. You have, no doubt, seen the grisly display in the window of Morgan's Hardware?"

"Yes, I've seen it," Dane replied.

"Even though your violence is...shall we say, justified, I can't help but wonder what we gain by replacing one form of violence with another."

"You ever seen anyone fight a forest fire?" Dane asked.

"No. You may have noticed we don't have a great deal of forest country around here."

"I've seen forest fires in the country north of here," Dane said. "Sometimes, the only way to stop one is to start another fire. They call it a backfire." Dane held up his two hands to demonstrate. "The fires burn together...then they go out. You lose some...but you save much more."

"I see what you mean," Pipkin said. "But what if someone were to be caught between the two fires?"

"He would get burned."

"Precisely, Mr. Calder. And the good citizens of

Rebel Ridge, it seems to me, are about to be caught between those two fires."

"Not if the good citizens of Rebel Ridge are the ones who start the backfire," Dane suggested.

"What do you mean?"

"I mean it's time for Rebel Ridge to fight back," Dane said. "If you don't want Lowman as your sheriff, kick him out."

Pipkin shook his head. "It isn't that easy, I'm afraid. We've discussed this very thing before, but we have been unable to come to a consensus as to how best to do it. That is why a few misguided businessmen, with the best of intentions perhaps, but certainly without the unanimous consent of the citizenry, hired you to fight out battle for us."

"Oh, but they didn't hire me," Dane replied. "I didn't accept the offer, remember?"

"Then why are you here?"

"Everyone has to be somewhere," Dane said.

"If you seriously believe that we should fight our own battle, then it would have been better if you hadn't come at all."

"Why?"

"Because the leaders of our fair community will leave it all up to you. Don't you see? Now there is even less of a chance that the town will stand up to Lowman and his gang."

"Oh? How about you? Would you have written that article if I hadn't come to town?"

"I...I don't know," Pipkin replied. "Anyway, look what it got me." He took in his office with a wave of his arm. "My press was overturned, my window was broken, and my type is so scattered that it will take me a week to get it straight again."

"Are you sorry you wrote the article, Mr. Pipkin?"

Pipkin stood there for a moment, resting his hand on the press. Finally he looked up at Dane.

"No, by god, I'm not," he answered. "I'm not a bit sorry."

"I was hoping you would say that," Dane said, smiling. "Because there is somethin' I want you to do for me."

Dane took out a piece of paper and handed it to Pipkin. "I want you to print this," he said.

Pipkin looked at the paper, then read aloud: "Fifty thousand dollars in new greenbacks to go from Girard to bank in Dudleyville. Specie to be transferred by courier on the seventeenth, instant." Pipkin looked up. "That's tomorrow," he said. "Are you sure you want this printed?"

"Yes, right in the middle of the front page," Dane said.

"But you must know that if Lowman reads this article, he's going to go there like flies to honey."

"Yes, that is what I believe," Dane said.

"Then I don't understand. Why would you...?" Pipkin stopped midsentence and smiled. "You want him to go after that money, don't you?"

"I figure that money will get Lowman and some of his gang out of town."

Pipkin scratched his cheek again, leaving yet another smear.

"No, I can't do that," he finally said.

"Why not? Don't you want to get rid of Lowman?"

"Of course I do. But I couldn't do this to the courier...set these people on him like that."

"That's the courier's worry, not yours."

"I won't do it to him."

Dane smiled. "Not even if I tell you I'm the courier?"

"You?"

"That's right."

"But you're just setting yourself up as bait. Don't you realize that?"

"If you want to catch a fox, you have to bait the trap," Dane said.

"Maybe that's true. But I've noticed something about bait."

"What's that?"

"Even when you catch the fox...the bait is nearly always eaten."

"I might be a little bigger mouthful than the fox can handle," Dane suggested.

Pipkin chuckled. "You know, you might be at that."

FOURTEEN

AFTER LEAVING THE NEWSPAPER OFFICE, DANE walked two doors down the street, then cut in between two buildings and climbed a set of outside stairs to an upstairs office. This was the office of Doc Frazer. There was a woman in the doctor's office and a small boy. The boy's mouth was open, and Doc was holding his tongue down with a wooden depressor as he studied the boy's throat.

"I'll be right with you," Doc said, hearing the jangling bell but not bothering to look around to see who had entered.

The boy's mother looked around to see who had just come in, and seeing Dane, gasped in quick fear. Dane used to be very self-conscious about this type of reaction, but he was used to it now. The stories that circulated about him were a by-product of his skills and efficiency. Many of the tales of his exploits, including those that demonstrated his fearlessness against overwhelming odds, were true. But there were other stories about him as well, stories that made him into an almost mythological figure, and it was these which tended to frighten women and children.

"How do you do, ma'am?" Dane said, smiling so disarmingly that, for a moment, the woman could forget who he was. The woman found herself smiling back and feeling a sense of daring as well as an unbidden and totally unexpected excitation.

"I am doing well, thank you, Mr. Calder," the woman said.

"It's nothing but a little congestion," Doc Frazer told the woman when he finished examining the boy. He handed her a small brown bottle. "This is a tonic of liverwort syrup and molasses. Give him about a table-spoon of this, three times a day, and the congestion will clear up."

"Thank you, Doctor," the woman said, taking the bottle, then reaching for her son. When she looked at Dane again, she was flustered. "It, uh, was nice to meet you, Mr. Calder," she said huskily.

"The pleasure was all mine," Dane replied.

"Well, I'll be," Doc Frazer said a moment later as the woman and her child were using the outside stairs that led down to the street. "I've known Mrs. Peterson for as long as I've been in Rebel Ridge and I've never known her to be anything but a fine, decent, upstanding woman. There's not a breath of scandal about her. Yet, the way she was just now..." Doc let the thought hang.

"Don't make anything out of it, Doc," Dane said easily. He chuckled. "I know *I've* tried a few times in the past, and *I* haven't been able to," he added.

"But the way she was looking at you," Doc said. "It was positively indecent."

"Like you said, Doc, she's a good wife and mother," Dane said. "When somebody like that sees someone like me, she gets a glimpse of the other side of the veil, that's all. You've seen a couple of horses when they've been separated by a fence, haven't you? The black horse has his neck stretched as far as it will go across the fence eatin' grass from the white horse's field, while the white horse has his neck across the fence, eatin' grass from the black horse's field."

Doc laughed. "Now that you bring it up, I suppose I have seen that. I guess, like all adages, 'The grass is always greener on the other side' has a degree of validity. But what brings you up here, Dane? I'm sure you didn't come in here to talk about old sayings."

"No, I didn't," Dane agreed. He walked over to the window in Doc's office and looked out onto the street. From here, he had a perfect view of the fount of the hardware store, and he could see the two coffins lying there for public viewing. There were still several people standing on the street, looking through the window at the display. "Doc, do you want your town back?" he asked.

"Yes," Doc answered quickly. "But I thought you weren't going to take our offer."

"I'm not," Dane said, turning around.

"Then, I don't understand," Doc said, his face mirroring his confusion. "How are we goin' to get it back?"

"You're goin' to take it back for yourselves," Dane suggested.

Doc laughed, self-deprecatingly. "I don't know," he said. "If you think we can do that, than you have more confidence in us than I."

"I'm going to help," Dane offered.

"Oh, well," Doc said, obviously relieved. "If you're goin' to be here with us then—"

"I'm not goin' to be here," Dane interrupted. "You're goin' to do it alone. I just said I would help."

"I don't understand," Doc said. "How are you goin' to help if you aren't here?"

"I'll explain it to you," Dane said. "But I only want to explain it once. Do you think you can get a few men together? I want good men, men who are dependable, and men you can trust."

"We have a lot of good, dependable, and trustworthy men in Rebel Ridge," Doc said. "It's no problem findin' them. But we don't have anyone who knows anything about guns. Why, even the least skilled of Lowman's deputies could take the measure of any of us in a gunfight."

"You let me worry about that," Dane said. "All I want you to do is get them together...in secret, if possible."

"We can meet in the upstairs room over Barnet's Store," Doc suggested, remembering where they had met when they'd made the decision to send for Dane in the first place. "George Barnet is as solid a citizen as we have in this town."

"That's exactly the kind of people we want," Dane said. He looked at the clock which hung on Doc Frazer's wall. "Can you have them there by noon?"

"I don't see why not," Doc said.

* * *

WHEN DANE CALDER arrived at the Barnet General Mercantile Store at noon, he saw that Doc Frazer had made good on his word. Besides Doc, there were seven others. Dane already knew Littlefield, Barnet, Pipkin, Parker, and Newberry. Now he was introduced to Jake Rankin, the town carpenter, and Ed Kotulla, who owned the leather goods store. Rankin was the youngest—Dane guessed he would be about twenty-five, and Littlefield, at fifty-five, was the oldest.

"All right, Dane, we're all here," Doc said.

"What do you have in mind?" Parker asked.

"Did Doc tell you anything?"

"Doc told us you had an idea about how we could take our town back," Littlefield said.

"That's right. You can take your town back if you are willin' to make the effort," Dane said.

"We'll make the effort," Rankin put in. "You lead us, and we'll do whatever you ask."

Dane shook his head.

"I won't be leadin' you," he said. "You are goin' to have to choose your leader from among your own."

"What? Wait a minute," Littlefield said. He looked at Doc. "What is this, Doc? I thought you said he was goin' to help us."

"I am goin' to help you," Dane said. "I just won't be leadin' you."

"Then who is goin' to lead us?"

"As I said, you'll have to choose one of your own."

"How do you expect us to do that?" Newberry

asked. "What do we know about guns and killin' and such? We're merchants."

"Yes. Merchants don't fight," one of the others said.

"Is that a fact? Gentlemen, it wasn't all that long ago that more than three million men just like you—farmers, lawyers, doctors, engineers, teamsters, railroaders—men from every occupation under the sun, including merchants," he added pointedly, "came together to form the mightiest army the world has ever seen. Some of you might remember the War between the States."

"I damn well remember it," Barnet said. "I was in it. I fought at Shiloh with the Fifteenth Ohio."

"How about that? I was at Shiloh too," Newberry said. He laughed. "Only I was with the Twelfth Mississippi. I reckon it's a good thing we didn't bump into each other then."

"And when you men were at Shiloh, did you do your duty?"

"I didn't skedaddle, if that's what you mean," Newberry said.

"I reckon I did my part," Barnet said.

"Yes, and so did hundreds of thousands of other men just like you. Do you see what I'm gettin' at? You don't need to be fast with a gun or have a mean streak. Armies are made up of men just like you...men with guts and determination. Barnet, you and Newberry have already shown that you have that. Now, what about the rest of you?"

"I figure if a million other men can do it, there's no reason why I can't," Rankin said.

"Same here," Kotulla replied. "You can count me in."

"Good," Dane replied. "Now, the first thing you have to do is select a leader."

"I figure it should be either Barnet or Newberry," Littlefield suggested. "They were both in the war, so they have a little experience in this sort of thing."

"Not me," Newberry said. "I mean I'll go along with the rest of you, and I'll do my share of the fightin', just like I done at Shiloh. But one thing I learned when I was in the Army was that I was a better private than anything else. What about you, Barnet? What rank was you?"

"I was a lieutenant by the time the war was over," Barnet said.

Newberry smiled. "Well, then that settles it. Lieutenant Barnet of the Yankee Army has my vote."

"Any objections from anyone?" Littlefield asked. When there were none, he smiled at Barnet. "It looks like you're our leader," he said.

"Good," Dane said. "Barnet, I want you to plan this like a military battle, because that's exactly what it's goin' to be. Get your men together, figure out a plan of attack, then attack. And I figure the best time to do it is tomorrow."

"Tomorrow?" Barnet replied. "No, that's too soon. We've got to have a few meetings, work out some—"

"No time for all that," Dane interrupted. "It has to be tomorrow."

"Why tomorrow?"

Pipkin smiled broadly. "I believe I know why it

must be done tomorrow," he said. "It's because tomorrow, Lowman will be gone."

"Gone? Gone where?" Littlefield asked.

"Well, if I were a bettin' man, I would say he is going to be waiting somewhere on the road to Dudleyville," Pipkin said. When it was obvious that no one else knew what he was talking about, Pipkin told them about the article he was printing, stating that fifty thousand dollars in new greenbacks was being transported by courier to the bank in Dudleyville.

"Fifty thousand dollars?" Kotulla said. He let out a low whistle. "That's more money than there is in the whole world."

Dane chuckled. "It's not more money than there is in the whole world," he said. "But it is a lot of money. I had to make it a lot of money in order to tempt Lowman. But, since the courier isn't goin' to be carryin' any money at all...it's as easy to say he's carryin' fifty thousand as it is to say he's carrying ten thousand."

"What are you talkin' about?" Newberry asked.

Barnet smiled broadly. "I think I know," he said. "You are goin' to be the courier, aren't you, Dane?"

Dane nodded.

"That's pretty good," Barnet said. "Yes, sir, that is pretty damn good."

"What's pretty good?" Rankin asked. "What are you talkin' about?"

"Don't you see, boys? As soon as Lowman reads that newspaper article, he's goin' to hightail it after that money shipment. Only, there is no money. Calder here is actin' as a decoy for us. He's goin' to draw Lowman out of town."

"Not only Lowman," Dane said. "Unless I miss my guess, He'll want two others with him. Any more and the split will be too little, any less, and he can't be sure he can get the job done."

"Which leaves the others for us," Barnet concluded.

"Think you can handle them?" Dane asked.

"I think we'll be ready," Barnet said. "What do you boys think?"

Pipkin smiled. "I say, give us our marchin' orders, Captain. The Rebel Ridge Volunteer Militia is ready to go to war."

* * *

"Jesse, you seen this?" Wooten asked, dropping the paper on Lowman's table.

Lowman, who was playing a game of solitaire, glanced up.

"What is it?" he grunted. "Another editorial from our fearless newspaperman?"

"Uh-uh, nothing like that," Wooten said. "Read this here story." Wooten pointed to an article on the front page.

Lowman glanced at it and then, when his interest was aroused, picked it up and began reading it. Not until he was finished with the article did he make a comment.

"Have you talked to anyone about this?" he asked.

"Not yet. I figured I would show it to you first."

"Good, good," Lowman said. He looked around the saloon and saw nearly half a dozen of his deputies in various pursuits...drinking, playing cards, or talking with the girls. He knew that at least two others, including Colby, had gone upstairs with a girl. "Get Bucky and the two of you come upstairs to my room. Don't let anyone know what's goin' on."

"What about Colby?"

"Especially not Colby," Lowman said.

"All right," Wooten replied. "I'll get 'im, and we'll be right there."

Lowman closed up the deck, then left his table and walked up the stairs to the second-floor landing.

"Jesse, you want to sit in here?" one of the deputies called.

Lowman yawned and stretched. "No, I think I'll get a little shut-eye," he answered. "Maybe later."

Once in his room, he rolled himself a cigarette, then waited until Bucky and Wooten showed up. They came in a few minutes later.

"Did anyone see you come up?" Lowman asked.

"No," Wooten replied.

"Anyway, what difference would it make?" Bucky asked. "These are our boys."

Lowman smiled, then shook his head. "Not for this, they ain't," he said.

"Not for what? What's goin' on, Jesse? All Wooten said was that you wanted to see us."

"Bucky, how would you like to have ten thousand dollars?" Lowman asked.

"Ten thousand dollars? Where would I get that kind of money?"

"I'm goin' to give it to you," Lowman said.

Bucky laughed, then frowned. "You got that kind of money, Jesse?" he asked.

"Not yet," Lowman admitted. "But after the three of us pull a little job, I will have. There's goin' to be ten thousand apiece for each of you."

"Wait until I tell the others," Bucky said, smiling broadly.

"No!" Lowman said quickly. "That's exactly what you aren't goin' to do. This one is just for us."

"How are we goin' to keep Colby from findin' out?" Bucky asked. "Seems like that sonofabitch knows ever'thing that goes on."

Lowman thought of Colby's taunting him over his trouble with women.

"Yeah," Lowman said. "Sometimes it does seem that way. So we'll just have to make certain that he doesn't find out, that's all. Wooten, you go around and gather up all the newspapers so he doesn't learn about the money shipment. And both of you, make certain you don't say one word about this."

"You can count on me, Jesse. I ain't sayin' nothing," Bucky promised.

"Me neither," Wooten added.

"All right, that takes care of that," Lowman said. "Now, according to the newspaper article, the money is being transferred from Girard to Dudleyville. That means the courier is going to have to pass through Fiddler's Draw. When he gets there, we'll be waiting for him. But if we're goin' to get there on time, we're goin' to have to get an early start, so we're goin' to slip out one at a time, early in the mornin'. We'll meet about three miles out of town." Lowman held up his finger. "And if either one of you aren't there, I'll go on without you. Think about that. If you sleep late, you'll be costin' yourself ten thousand dollars."

"I'll be there," Bucky promised.

"Me too," Wooten added.

FIFTEEN

BOB WOOTEN LEFT FIRST, RIDING OUT OF REBEL Ridge at about six a.m. the next morning. Bucky left around eight and Lowman at about eight-thirty. Newberry watched them all leave. Had Newberry not been at the citizens' meeting the day before, he would have been as much in the dark as Frank Colby and the dozen or so deputies who remained behind.

As soon as Lowman left, however, Newberry hurried down to the mercantile store to give Barnet the news.

"All right," Barnet said with a look of grim determination on his face. "This is what we've been waiting for." Barnet looked over at the clock on his wall. "Newberry, you pass the word to all the deputies that Lowman wants a meeting with them in your saloon at ten o'clock. We must have all of them in there then. And also—this is important—make sure that no one else except the deputies are in the saloon."

"What about the girls?" Newberry said. "They'll still be asleep at ten."

"I don't know. I hate leavin' them in there, but if they all leave it could cause someone to get suspicious."

"Actually, I think I can sneak the girls out the back way," Newberry said. "But it's the other customers I'm worried about. I sure can't take them through the back without arousing suspicion."

Barnet stroked his chin for a moment. "Yeah," he said. "I see what you mean." Suddenly he smiled. "Say, I've got an idea. Why don't you have the deputies run the customers out for you?"

"How? What do you mean?"

"It's simple. You just post a sign that reads, 'By order of Sheriff Lowman, the saloon is closed to all citizens today.' If the deputies think that's what Lowman wants, they'll do it for you."

Newberry laughed. "Yeah," he said. "Yes, I believe that would do it."

"I'll get all the others together. We'll meet at Morgan's Hardware. You come down and join us as soon as you can get away. And Newberry?"

"Yeah?" Newberry asked, looking back.

"Be armed," Barnet said.

Newberry smiled. "You're damn right I will be," he said. "I've been waitin' on this a long time."

Barnet watched Newberry leave, then went to the back of the store, into the area of the building which served as the living quarters for himself, his wife, and his two children. He dragged an old trunk out from beneath the bed. Opening the lid, he began going through all the items which had, long ago, been so carefully packed inside. There was the dress Josie had worn when they were married...the christening gown worn by both children at their baptisms...a wool shawl passed down from his grandmother and said to have been made by some ancient relative in the old county. Finally he found what he was looking for.

"George?" a woman's voice called softly.

Barnet turned around to see his wife standing in the doorway. "George, what is it?" she asked. "Why are you looking around in the trunk?"

"What are you doin' back here, Josie? One of us has to watch the store."

"Never you mind the store, George Barnet," his wife said. "Something is going on, and I want to know what it is. You had that mysterious meeting yesterday. Mr. Newberry was just over here, and now you're going out again." She saw what he was holding in his hand. "What are you doing? That's your old Army uniform, isn't it?"

"Yes, it is," George said. He sniffed it, and it smelled of cedar and mothballs. He held up the light blue pants and the dark blue jacket. On its shoulders were the red shoulder boards of an artillery lieutenant. "I wonder if I can still get into it." He stripped off his shirt, then stuck his arms into the sleeves of the jacket.

"George Barnet, I want to know what is going on," his wife insisted.

Barnet smiled when he found that he could still get the jacket buttoned. "Look at this, Josie," he said. "It's a perfect fit."

Barnet's wife began to sob quietly. When Barnet saw her, he went over and put his arms around her. "What's wrong?" he asked.

"That's what I want to know," she said. "George, you are frightening me. I asked you what is going on and you won't tell me."

Barnet sighed. "All right, Josie, I'll tell you, but you must promise to say nothing about it, do you understand? Say nothing to no one, for if you do speak about it, you could put several people's lives in danger...including mine."

"George, you are making me even more frightened," she said. "What have you done?"

"It's not what I have done," Barnet replied. "It's what I am goin' to do...or rather, what *we* are goin' to do. We're takin' back our town."

"Taking back our town? What do you mean? And who is 'we'?"

"Littlefield, Newberry, Doc Frazer, a few others, and me," Barnet said. "Josie, we're goin' to run Lowman and those rascal deputies out."

"George, no," his wife pleaded. "Let someone else worry about that. You're not a lawman...you're a store clerk."

Barnet looked hard at his wife. "Woman," he said. "I served very proudly under a store clerk at Shiloh. His name was U. S. Grant, and when he was needed, he answered the call. Now, give me your prayers or your silence...but stay out of my way!"

Josie put her arms around him. "I'm frightened," she said.

"That's understandable," Barnet replied. "Anytime

a man goes off to war, he leaves behind a family who is frightened for him. But that doesn't stop him from doin' his duty. You remember how it was."

"That was different. We were both very young then, and there were no children."

"Believe me, life was just as precious then as it is now," Barnet said. He brushed a fall of hair back from her forehead and kissed her there. "Don't be frightened," he said. "This is somethin' that must be done."

Josie took a deep breath, then nodded. "I know it is," she finally said. "And I'm very proud of you for doing it. But that doesn't stop me from being afraid."

Barnet picked up a bow and a quiver of arrows.

"Oh, George, you aren't going to try and fight those gunmen with a bow and arrow?" Josie asked, aghast.

Barnet smiled. "That's exactly what I'm goin' to do," he said. "I hope they don't expect much either. Now, don't be frightened for me, do you hear? I'll come back to you without a scratch. I promise you." He put on his campaign hat, and then, carrying his bow and the quiver of arrows, went out through the back door so he could go to Morgan's Hardware by way of the alley.

* * *

OVER IN THE Silver Strike Saloon, Colby was still asleep when one of the girls knocked on his door and began calling quietly for Hattie Mae. Hattie Mae had spent the night in Colby's bed and was now lying beside him, snoring softly. Though she was the one being called, Colby was the one who was awakened.

"What do you want?" Colby called.

"Mr. Colby, I need to see Hattie Mae. Would you send her out, please?"

"Yeah, yeah, take her," Colby grumbled. He pushed on Hattie Mae's shoulder. Of all the girls in the place, she was always the hardest to wake up. "Get up, woman," he said.

Hattie Mae woke up. "What is it?" she asked.

"I don't know, somebody wants you out there."

"Umm, and I was sleepin' so good. Tell her to come back."

"You were snorin' like a hog," Colby growled. "Get on out there and see what she wants. Maybe that way I can get a little rest."

"Do you want me to come back, sweetie?"

"No," Colby growled. He liked having a woman at night, but he didn't care that much for them the next morning. "Be gone with you."

Hattie Mae slipped into her clothes quickly, then stepped out of the room. Colby heard them whispering about something outside and put the pillow over his head to block them out. Whatever they had to say couldn't possibly be important enough to interrupt his sleep.

Colby did manage to go back to sleep, though it didn't last long, for sometime later there was a loud, impatient knocking on the door, followed by a man's gruff voice.

"Colby! Colby, are you asleep?" an insistent voice called.

"Who the hell can sleep with all this bangin' and yellin'?" Colby replied irritably.

Colby got out of bed and walked over to the door. When he jerked it open, he saw Jacobs standing there.

"Dammit all to hell, Jacobs, what's goin' on around here this mornin'?" he asked. "First the damn women wake me up, and now you. What do you want?"

"Lowman has called a meeting for ever'body at ten o'clock," Jacobs said. "It's pert' near that now."

"A meetin'? I didn't hear nothin' about a meetin'. What's it about?"

"I don't know," Jacobs said. "But it must be important. I've never known him to call any meetings before."

Colby ran a hand through his tousled hair, then scratched his chin. "All right," he said. "All right, tell 'im to hold his horses. I'll be down there in a few minutes."

Colby poured some water from the pitcher into the basin and splashed some of it onto his face. Then he got dressed, pulled on his boots, and strapped on his gun.

As Colby reached for his hat, he happened to look out through the window. His room was upstairs and in the back of the saloon, so the window didn't open onto the street, but through the alley opening, he could see some of the street, and what he saw puzzled him. He saw Rankin and Littlefield going into the closed hardware store. Seeing two of the local businessmen going into a closed store wasn't, in itself, curious. But both Littlefield and Rankin were carrying rifles...and Colby did find that mildly curious.

Putting that aside, he finally went downstairs, where he saw all the deputies sitting around the tables, talking quietly among themselves. He noticed, with some irritation, that neither Lowman nor Bucky was here. If Lowman wanted to call a meeting, Colby thought, the least he could do would be to show up.

Colby walked over to the bar, then looked up and down for the barkeep.

"Newberry," he called. "Newberry, you back there?"

"Newberry ain't here," one of the deputies said.

Colby turned his back to the bar. "Where is he?" he asked.

"I don't know."

Colby looked around the saloon. It was exceptionally quiet, and except for the deputies, no one else was here. There was something not quite right about things, and Colby scratched his chin.

"What is this?" he asked. "What's goin' on?"

"I don't know," Jacobs answered. "All I know is, we got word that Lowman wanted a meeting with all of us, an' he posted that sign over there tellin' ever'one else to stay away."

"There's somethin'..." Colby started to say, but he was so unable to put his finger on what was bothering him that he couldn't even form the words to express his concern. As a result, he let the sentence dangle, uncompleted.

"What?" Jacobs asked, totally unaware of anything untoward about the situation.

"Nothing," Colby said. "I need a drink, that's all." With Newberry absent, Colby walked around behind the bar to pour his own liquor. He stood back there for a moment while he tossed half his drink down.

"All right, we're here," he said. "So where the hell is Lowman?"

"I don't know, he ain't showed up yet."

"What about Bucky? Don't he have to make the meeting?"

"He ain't here either."

"Neither is Wooten," one of the other deputies replied. "I went to get him over to the livery…Wooten has a room there, but he wasn't nowhere around."

"Jacobs, go up and knock on Lowman's door," Colby said.

"Not me," Jacobs replied. "Lowman don't like being woke up early in the morning."

"I said go up and knock on his door," Colby repeated, his words cold and demanding.

"All right, all right, you don't have to get into a huff over it," Jacobs said, holding up his hands as if warding Colby off. "I'll do it, but I'm goin' to tell him it was you made me do it."

Colby walked over to the batwing doors and looked out onto the street. He didn't see anyone…not one wagon, horse, or pedestrian. He looked toward Morgan's Hardware but saw nothing there either. Finally he tossed down the rest of his drink, then walked back to the bar to pour himself another one.

"What day is today?" he asked. "Is this Sunday?"

"Sunday? No, it's Thursday, I think. Or maybe Friday," someone answered. "Why?"

"I don't know," Colby said. "It just seems awful quiet to me for some reason."

Jacobs came back down the stairs.

"When's he comin' down?" Colby asked.

"I don't know."

"What do you mean, you don't know? Didn't you ask him?"

"I couldn't ask him, Colby. There weren't no one in his room. There ain't no one in Bucky's room, neither."

"What the hell is goin' on around here?" Colby asked. He moved quickly up the stairs to Lowman's room. "Lowman?" he called. "Lowman, you up here?"

He pushed open the door to Lowman's room and saw that, as Jacobs had said, it was empty. Then he smiled. Lowman was probably with one of the women, and with his "problem," Colby thought to himself, he was probably having a hard time of it. "Or maybe it's not so hard," he said out loud. "Yeah, maybe that's the problem." He laughed aloud at his own joke.

"Lowman, are you down there with one of the women?" he called, walking down toward the end of the hall where the five women had their rooms. He knocked on the first woman's door, and when he got no answer, he pushed it open. Like Lowman's room, this one was empty.

"Hattie Mae?" Colby called. He knew Hattie Mae was here...she'd just left his room a short time ago. "Hattie Mae, where the hell are you?"

Colby pushed open the door to Hattie Mae's room, but she was gone too. So was Clara, and so were the other girls. The entire top floor was empty.

"What the hell is goin' on here?" Colby muttered again. He started to go back out into the hallway, but just as he did, something outside the window got his attention. He thought he had seen someone moving on the roof of the leather goods store across the street.

"You're a dumb sonofabitch to be patchin' your roof in the heat of the day," he said, moving over to the window for another look.

At first, there was no one there, and he started to turn away. But then he saw another movement on the roof of the apothecary.

"What the hell? Are two of you patchin' your roof?" he asked. He stayed by the window for a long moment, continuing to look outside, then saw one of them move again. This time he got a very good look at him. The man on the roof was Kotulla, and he wasn't carrying patching material. Like Littlefield and Rankin before him, he was carrying a rifle. Suddenly it all came together and Colby knew what was going on.

"Son...of...a...bitch!" he said aloud. He darted out of the room and bolted down the stairs. "Get your guns!" he shouted. "Get your guns! We're about to be attacked!"

SIXTEEN

"WHAT ARE YOU TALKING ABOUT, ATTACK?" JACOBS asked. "Who's attacking us? Indians?" he laughed.

"No, dammit, the town is," Colby said. "Hell, half the damn town is crawlin' around out there on roofs and behind the buildings. And they've all got rifles."

Jacobs walked over to the batwing doors to look outside. At that precise moment, he saw someone with a rifle looking out one of the upstairs hotel rooms.

"Sonofabitch! He's right!" Jacobs yelled. He drew his pistol and shot toward the hotel. His bullet punched a hole in the glass window, but other than that, it did no damage.

"What did you shoot for, you dumb bastard?" Colby shouted.

"What are you talking about? I seen someone in the hotel window with a rifle pointed toward us," Jacobs answered.

"As long as they thought they had us in the dark,

we had the advantage," Colby said. "Now they know that we know."

"So what? There ain't nothing out there but a bunch of ribbon clerks and storekeeps," Jacobs replied. "Why don't we just go out there and...unnh!"

Jacobs's sentence was cut short by a bullet fired from a rifle from somewhere across the street. The bullet caught him high in the chest and spun him around. Spewing out a little fountain of blood, he put his hand up to the wound to stanch the flow, but the blood streamed through his fingers. He looked up with an expression of surprise on his face.

"A ribbon clerk," he said. "Who would've thought?"

"Get these tables turned over, men," Colby shouted. "Get 'em up to the windows! We've got a fight on our hands!"

* * *

GEORGE BARNET WAS CLIMBING up onto the roof of the hardware store when he heard the shooting start. He hurried to get there, but as he was carrying the box and arrows and a heavy box, his movement was somewhat restricted. He was a little aggravated because the shooting wasn't supposed to start until he gave the command, and as soon as he got onto the roof, he mentioned it.

"We couldn't help it, George," Littlefield replied. "They must've seen us. They started the shootin'."

"All right, it doesn't matter," Barnet said. "The ball is opened now. It's up to us to give them all they can handle. Help me with these, will you?"

"Sure, George. What do you want me to do?"

Barnet opened the lid of the case he was carrying, revealing the contents. It was an entire case of dynamite sticks.

"Start tyin' them onto the arrows," he said. "About here." He indicated where the sticks should go.

For the next few minutes, bullets flew overhead as Barnet and Littlefield worked to tie the dynamite sticks to the arrows. When they had about ten of them done, Barnet lit a cigar, then handed it to Littlefield.

"You light them," he said. "I'll shoot them."

Smiling, Littlefield held the hot end of the cigar to the dynamite fuse. "Consolidated Mining never saw its dynamite put to a better use," he said.

When the fuse was sputtering, Barnet raised up and shot the arrow toward the front of the saloon. It fell short, landing in the water trough just in front. A moment later, the dynamite went off, splintering the trough and throwing up a shower of water.

"I didn't compensate enough for the weight of the dynamite stick," Barnet said, picking up a second arrow. "I'll put this one inside."

With the second fuse sputtering, Barnet raised up to loose another arrow. A fine stream of smoke marked the path of the arrow from the roof of the hardware store, across the street, then through the front window of the saloon, right between the letter r on Silver and the letter S in Strike. A moment later there was an explosion inside the saloon which blew out the windows and sent the batwing doors flying out into the street.

Four deputies came outside then, firing as they ran. They were cut down by a hail of bullets from the citizen army.

"Cease-fire!" Barnet shouted. "Cease-fire!"

The firing stopped, and for a moment, there was absolute silence. Then, as the members of the citizen army realized they had won, they began to cheer.

Doc Frazer was the first one to go down onto the street, where, once again, the doctor, he began examining the bodies to see if anyone was left alive. The others joined him in the street, laughing and talking about their victory, happy and proud that, once again, the town belonged to them.

"I'd better check inside the saloon," Doc said. "There may be some wounded in there."

"I'm goin' to go back up and get the dynamite off the roof," Barnet said. "If it stays out in the sun and gets too hot, it might go off."

"Yeah, we don't want to destroy another building," Newberry said. "I'm goin' to need all of you to help me rebuild mine."

Barnet, feeling a sense of pride, accomplishment, and relief that he had not felt since the day the war ended, climbed back onto the roof of the hardware store. He had just closed the lid of the box holding the dynamite when he heard the sound of a pistol shot. Startled, he hurried over to the edge of the roof to see what had happened.

Doc Frazer came out of the saloon, walked out into the middle of the street, then collapsed.

"Someone shot the doc!" somebody yelled.

Barnet wondered who could have done it. He

thought everyone was dead. The mystery was solved when he saw Frank Colby come out of the saloon, apparently unhurt by the blast that had gone off inside. Colby was holding a pistol in his hand, which gave him an advantage over every member of the citizen army. Most of them had left their rifles behind, thinking the battle was over. Rankin and Parker had their rifles with them, but they were holding them loosely by their sides.

"Well, now," Colby said. "You fellas had yourself quite a little party here, didn't you? Well, the party's over. But you've left me with a little problem. There are five of you and I have only four bullets left. Who will I kill and who will I spare?" He smiled evilly.

"I know, I'll spare the undertaker. After all, someone will have to bury the dead." He pointed his pistol at Littlefield. "You first, Littlefield. I'm sure you are the one who organized this little get-together."

Colby pulled the hammer back on his pistol and aimed carefully at Littlefield. Littlefield began shaking, but he didn't say a word. For a moment there was an eerie tableau vivant, with everyone paying such close attention to the drama being performed that no one saw the little plume of smoke zip down from the roof across the street. Not until the arrow buried itself in Colby's chest did they become aware of what had just happened.

"Get down!" Barnet shouted from the roof.

Colby clutched at the arrow in his chest, attempting to pull it out. Then he suddenly realized that his troubles were much more serious than just the arrow itself, for tied to the arrow was a stick of dynamite, its fuse sputtering.

Colby's eyes grew wide in recognition and horror.

"No!" he shouted.

The others dived for the ground just as the stick of dynamite went off.

* * *

DANE HAD BEEN aware that three men were dogging him, riding parallel with him. Actually, he knew this more from some extra sense than from any direct observation, for the men trailing him were so good at their job he had not yet seen them. He also knew when they left him, riding ahead of him in order to get into position to set up the ambush, even though he did not see them leave, any more than he had seen them when they were following.

Dane didn't need to see them to know they were there and he didn't need to see them to know who they were. He knew it was Lowman and whoever Lowman had decided to bring along with him.

Several times during the ride Dane had stopped and lifted his canteen from the pommel to take a drink of water. Each time he stopped he would shove the cork back, then rehang his canteen. After that he would wipe the back of his hand across his mouth and stand in the stirrups to look around nervously. Each of these carefully staged episodes would conclude with him sitting back down and patting the bulging saddlebags.

All this was for the benefit of his shadows. While

he actually did look around each time, he was really only pretending to be nervous. And the patting of the bulging saddlebags was strictly for effect. He wanted Lowman to believe that fifty thousand dollars in greenbacks were being transported, just as the newspaper article had stated. In fact, there was no money at all. From the planted newspaper article to the feigned nervousness on the trail, it was all a ruse.

One of the reasons Dane had chosen this particular route was because there was only one obvious place for an ambush. The thing about ambushes, however, was the fact that they only worked when they were a complete surprise. If the ambushers were themselves surprised, then the whole thing could be turned around. And that was exactly what Dane planned to do.

The ambush point was just ahead, where the trail squeezed down to a narrow path going through a needle-like draw. At the other end of the draw a real courier would be a sitting duck. Since Lowman and whoever was with him had gone on ahead of Dane some time ago, Dane knew that they were waiting for him now.

When Dane reached the draw he knew that for the next several seconds he would be out of the line of sight of those who were waiting for him. This, then, was where he would have to make his move. As he passed under a large rock outcropping, he stood in his saddle, found a good handgrip, then pulled himself up into the rocks. Once in the rocks, he was able to climb over the top of the pass while his horse continued on through.

He ran at a crouch to the far end of the pass. From there, he could hear the slow, measured clop of his horse's hooves echoing through the long, narrow canyon. He pulled his pistol and waited...just as he knew Lowman was doing.

The sound of the hoof beats came closer until they were almost upon him.

"Now!" somebody suddenly shouted, and the narrow chasm was filled with the sound of exploding gunshots and whistling bullets.

Dane's horse, riderless of course, bolted out of the canyon.

"Grab the horse!" Lowman shouted. "The money's in the saddlebags!"

Bucky stepped in front of the horse and threw his arms up. The horse slid to a stop, its iron hooves striking sparks on the rocky ground. It reared defiantly, but Bucky's action had effectively stopped the bolt.

Bucky grabbed the halter and the horse grew still.

"All right, hold him, hold him!" Lowman shouted.

Dane had not yet been seen by the outlaws, so he was able to observe everything without himself being observed. He saw now that the third man in the little group was Bob Wooten.

"Hey! Where's the courier?" Wooten asked.

"We must've hit him," Lowman said. "He's prob'ly lyin' back there on the trail."

"Let the sonofabitch lie there," Bucky said. "We've got the money, that's all we need."

"No," Lowman said. "I left a man once before and he didn't die. This time I aim to finish the job."

"I'm glad to see that you are a man who learns from his mistakes, Lowman," Dane said, suddenly standing up.

"Damn! It's Calder!" Wooten said, raising his pistol.

Dane dropped Wooten with one well-placed shot. Bucky, thinking that Dane was preoccupied with Wooten, tried to take advantage of the fact. The shot which dropped Bucky was so close on the heels of the first that the two sounded almost as one. When Dane looked toward Lowman, he saw that the outlaw had both hands up in the air.

"I ain't makin' no fight of it, Calder," Lowman said. "Do you see? I've got my hands straight up in the air. I ain't makin' no fight of it."

* * *

IT WAS EARLY EVENING, though not yet dark when Dane led the little party back into Rebel Ridge. Lowman, looking sullen, was bound hands and feet in his saddle. Bucky and Wooten, both dead, were belly-down across theirs. Dane noticed the difference in the town, even before he saw the damaged saloon. There were people on the street, more people than he had ever seen on the streets of Rebel Ridge before. And they were laughing and animated. As he passed by Morgan's Hardware he saw why. There, in the front window, not in coffins but tied to boards, were the bodies of seven deputies. When Dane pulled up in front of the sheriff's office, he was met by Barnet and

Littlefield. Doc Frazer was there as well, but his arm was in a sling.

"Looks like a few changes have been made," Dane said as he swung down from the saddle.

"I'd say a few," Littlefield said. He saw Lowman sitting there, then the two bodies. "And with these galoots, it's complete," he added.

"I didn't see Colby."

Littlefield laughed. "And you won't," he said. "There's not enough left of him to see."

Dane looked over toward the saloon. "It does sort of look like you called out your artillery."

"What are we going to do with Lowman?" Littlefield asked.

"Why, hell, we're goin' to hang him," Dane said easily.

"Hang him?"

"That's what generally happens to the people I bring in," he said.

"Dane, we can't hang him," Barnet said.

"Are you getting squeamish on me?" Dane asked.

"Squeamish? No, it ain't that," Barnet said. He stroked his chin. "It's just that...well, we took our town back from Lowman because he was lawless. I don't want to see us become the same thing, and hangin' him without a trial would be nothing more than a lynchin'."

Dane nodded toward the hardware store. "You got seven bodies lying in the front window back there, don't you? Did you have a trial for them?"

"No, but that was different," Doc Frazer said. "We were the same as at war with them."

"Nobody ever gets hung during a war?"

"Sure—spies, murderers, and the like," Barnet said.

"All right, there's your legal justification," Dane said. "The town of Rebel Ridge raised a militia and elected you its commander. Until all the trouble is over, I'd say Rebel Ridge was under martial law, wouldn't you?"

"I don't know," Barnet mused.

"George, I think a very good case could be made for that," Littlefield interjected. "We damn well better be able to—otherwise even the killing of the deputies isn't legal."

"All right," Barnet said. "I suppose we were under martial law."

"*Are* under martial law," Dane corrected. "Martial law won't be lifted until it's all over with, and it won't be all over until Lowman is tried. As the commander, all you have to do is convene a court, select a jury, and appoint a prosecutor and counselor for the defense."

Lowman's face grew as gray as dust. "You can't do this to me," he said. "You got no right to do somethin' like this."

"On the contrary, sir," Brandon L. Pipkin spoke up. He had been standing to the side, listening to the entire conversation. "You see, you, yourself, have already established the precedence of a court in this town. With martial law in effect, the commander of the militia, in this case George Barnet, has every right and legal justification to utilize the court thus established to carry out the edicts of his military government. I have no doubt but that any decision such a court makes would be upheld...all the way up to and including the Supreme Court of the United States."

"Mr. Pipkin," Barnet said. "Would you act as prosecutor in this case?"

"I would be pleased to do so," Pipkin said.

"And you, Lowman," Barnet said, "may choose as your defense attorney, anyone you want."

"Ha! A fat choice I have," Lowman said. He looked into the faces of all the men gathered there in front of the sheriff's office, then suddenly broke out in a broad, evil smile. "All right. I choose Dane Calder."

"Calder can't defend you," Barnet said. "He knows damn well you are guilty."

"That doesn't matter," Pipkin spoke up. "It isn't necessary the defense lawyer believe his client is innocent. It is only necessary that the lawyer provides the best defense possible under the circumstances."

"Mr. Calder, would you defend this man to the best of your ability?" Barnet asked.

Dane looked at Lowman for a long moment before he answered. "Yeah," he finally said. "I will."

"All right, gentlemen," Barnet said. "Pipkin will prosecute, Calder will defend, and I will act as judge. Court will convene at Morgan's Hardware in one hour."

* * *

THOUGH THE TRIAL began just a little over an hour later, the entire town had gotten word of it, so that nearly the entire population was squeezed into the empty hardware store to watch. The fact that the seven bodies had not been removed and were still standing their ghostly watch from the front window added a touch of the macabre to the proceedings.

Pipkin opened the argument for prosecution, charging Lowman with terrorizing a town, with complicity in the murder of Parson Jorgenson and two other citizens who had been shot by his deputies while "resisting arrest," and with the direct murder of the cowboy Eli Underhill through an act of illegal hanging.

Pipkin called Newberry to the stand to testify with regard to the shooting of Parson Jorgenson. Newberry told how Truitt and Fontaine had come into his saloon on the day they arrived for the purpose of becoming Lowman's deputies.

"Did you witness the shooting of Parson Jorgenson?" Pipkin asked.

"Yes, I did," Newberry answered.

"Please tell us in your own words what happened."

Newberry told how both men began drinking, and how Truitt, intrigued by Jorgenson's hat, bet that he could shoot it off. Fontaine took him up on the bet and the tragic result was that Truitt missed the hat and hit Jorgenson between the eyes. Afterward, he claimed it was an accident and Lowman made no effort to punish him for what was, clearly, murder.

"Mr. Newberry, was Lowman in the saloon at the time?" Pipkin asked.

"Yes."

"Did he make any effort to stop Truitt from shooting?"

"No, he did not."

"Thank you. No further questions."

"Mr. Newberry, you were in the saloon, weren't you?" Dane asked.

"Yes, I was."

"Did you make any attempt to stop Truitt from shootin'?"

"No."

"Why not?"

"For one thing, it wasn't my place. And for another, I was afraid that if I tried to stop him, he would turn on me."

"Thank you. No more questions."

Pipkin jumped up again. "If you were afraid, why didn't you go to the sheriff? He was right there, wasn't he?"

"Yes, but in somethin' like that, I knew he wouldn't help me," Newberry answered.

"Thank you," Pipkin said. "Your Honor, prosecution calls Jarred Littlefield."

Pipkin questioned Littlefield about the murder of Eli Underhill. Littlefield explained how he had watched the young cowboy be placed on the back of a buckboard, then how the noose was slipped around his neck, and finally how the buckboard team was caused to dash forward, jerking the buckboard out from under Underhill's feet and causing him to be hanged.

"Mr. Littlefield," Dane said during the cross-examination, "when Eli Underhill was hanged, was it by a large, unruly mob?"

"No, not really."

"Who was present?"

"The sheriff and all his deputies."

"How would you describe the proceedings?"

"Cold, calculating, mechanical, and frightening," Littlefield said.

"Have you ever seen a hanging you considered legal, Mr. Littlefield?"

"Yes, I have."

"How would you describe it?"

"Well...cold, calculating, mechanical, and frightening," Littlefield said, realizing that he was using the same words of description.

"Then, in your mind, the only thing that was different about this hanging was that you don't believe it was legal?"

"I know it wasn't legal."

"But it was prescribed by the court, wasn't it?"

"By Lowman's court."

"But it was a court. It was not a mob lynching," Dane insisted.

"I suppose you could call it that."

"Thank you. No further questions."

As Lowman refused to testify in his own behalf, the case was over except for summation. Dane stood up and faced the jury that had been selected from among the townspeople.

"Gentlemen of the jury, the defendant, Jesse Lowman, is not the kind of man you would want as a neighbor, or a friend, and certainly, not as an enemy. He is a man who has lived for many years by the gun, and there is no doubt in my mind that he has killed many men. But we are not tryin' him for livin' by the gun nor for killing many men. We are bringing him to trial for some very specific charges...as an accomplice in the murder of Parson Jorgenson, and for the murder of Eli Underhill.

"If that is all we can find to try him on, then I've got some bad news for you. You can't find him guilty of that. He is no more an accomplice in the murder of Parson Jorgenson than is Newberry. Both were present at the time of the shooting, but that is all. Neither of them pulled the trigger, caused the trigger to be pulled, or encouraged Truitt to pull the trigger.

"And as for Eli Underhill, all you have to do is recall the testimony of Jarred Littlefield to see that it wasn't murder, it was a court-authorized execution. And, gentlemen of the jury, whether you agree with that court's decision or not...it was court-authorized. But, what court? You might well ask. I will answer for you. It is the same court we are in now, gentlemen, for according to Mr. Pipkin, the prosecutor in this case, the very legality of what we are doing now is based upon the establishment of a court in this town by Sheriff Jesse Lowman. We cannot find his court illegal without finding ourselves illegal. We can't have it both ways." Dane looked over at Lowman, who was now smiling smugly. "Lowman is guilty of a lot of things...but he isn't guilty of the charges that have been filed against him today."

Pipkin, who had thought perhaps that Dane Calder would mount a listless defense, sat at the prosecutor's table for a full moment, stunned by the effectiveness of Dane's argument. Finally, he stood up and walked over to address the jury.

"Gentlemen of the jury," he said. "Mr. Calder has, indeed, given us something to consider. He has said that we cannot find Jesse Lowman's court illegal without finding ourselves illegal. And there is merit to his argument, for, in the final analysis, we must be certain that what we are doing is not only legally, but morally right.

"Can we use this court to try Jesse Lowman? And if this court finds Lowman guilty, and sentences him to death by hanging, can we carry out that terrible sentence without permanent damage to our legal status as a civilized community, and to our immortal souls?"

Pipkin crossed his arms to study the jury and saw that, to a man, he had their rapt attention.

"The answer to that question is...yes. We can act as a court. Because you see, gentlemen, the court itself is not on trial here. What is on trial here is the perversion of that court, as was perpetrated by one man... Jesse Lowman. You can find Lowman guilty of perverting the court to commit the murder of Eli Underhill, while at the same time you affirm the sanctity of the court itself. Therefore I ask you to find a verdict of guilty. Thank you."

George Barnet, still in his military uniform and now acting as judge of the court, turned to the jury. "The jury may now retire to deliberate," he said.

It took the jury a half hour to find a verdict. During that deliberation, Pipkin came over to talk to Dane.

"I was very impressed at the defense you put up for Lowman," he said. "I thought you would just roll over."

Dane shook his head. "Hangin' someone is a

serious business," he said. "Anyone who is involved in it, no matter what part of it, has to treat it that way." He nodded toward Lowman. "If he didn't get the best defense I could possibly give him, you people would carry the guilt of hangin' him to your graves. This way...if the jury finds him guilty...and if he is hanged, there will be no second thoughts."

"The jury is comin' back," someone shouted from the rear of the building, and everyone took their seats to await the verdict. When the jury was seated, Barnet looked toward them.

"Has the jury reached a verdict?"

"We have, Your Honor," Rankin said, stepping forward. "And I have been selected to speak for it."

"How find you?"

Rankin cleared his throat. "To the charge of accomplice in the murder of Parson Jorgenson, we find the defendant...not guilty."

There were several gasps and groans of protest from those in the audience, and Barnet, using a carpenter's hammer as a gavel, banged on the table several times for order. Lowman smiled broadly.

"Maybe I had you all wrong, Calder," he said. "What do you say after this is over, me and you get together like I suggested when you first come here?"

Dane glared at Lowman.

"How find you to the second charge?" Barnet asked Rankin.

"To the charge of murder of Eli Underhill, we find the defendant...guilty."

This time the audience erupted into cheers and applause, and again, Barnet had to bang his gavel for quiet. Finally, with the audience silent, Barnet cleared his throat.

"Thank you, gentlemen of the jury," he said. "You are now dismissed. Would the prisoner please stand?"

Glaring now, Lowman stood.

"Jesse Lowman, you have been tried by this court, established under the effect of martial law and presided over by me as the commander of the militia. This court has found you guilty of murder in the first degree and I therefore sentence you to be hanged by the neck until you are dead. Sentence is to be carried out tomorrow morning. Please escort the prisoner across the street to the jail. This court is adjourned."

As two men stepped up to grab Lowman in compliance with Barnet's instructions, Lowman looked over toward Dane.

"Come around tomorrow, Calder. I'll try and do a fine dance for you," Lowman said.

Dane shook his head. "My job is over," he said. "I never watch the hangings."

"I see. It's just collect your money and go, is that it?"

"What money?" he asked. "Lowman, you never were important enough for anyone to put a price on your miserable hide."

"Then, I don't get it. Why did you do this? Why did you come after me like you done?"

Dane smiled. "Why, Lowman, I thought you knew," he said. "Sometimes a man does somethin' just for the fun of it."

A Look At: Orphan Cowboy

In the heart of Texas, an unexpected legacy shapes one man's destiny.

Lee Edward Holt, raised in the embrace of Our Lady of Mercy Orphanage, cherishes the only home he's ever known. Unaware of his true parentage, he thrives within the familiar walls of his upbringing—until he uncovers a shocking truth.

Stepping into the vast expanse of Kerr County, Texas, the discovered existence of Lee Edward's biological family awakens in him a sense of belonging. With a living mother and the late owner of Long Trail Ranch revealed as his father, he inherits an expansive 85,000-acre ranch alongside his stepsister, Mary Beth Hunter.

When a neighboring ranch threatens their land, Lee Edward takes it upon himself to partake in a daring cattle drive to save his family's legacy. And in a breathtaking twist of events, he ends up on a perilous balloon flight, facing challenges that test the very fabric of his Texan spirit.

Will Lee Edward's newfound love and the bonds forged on Long Trail Ranch be enough to conquer the challenges that lie ahead, or will this orphan cowboy's legacy slip through his fingers once and for all?

AVAILABLE NOW

About the Author

Robert Vaughan sold his first book when he was nineteen. That was several years and nearly five-hundred books ago. Since then, he has written the novelization for the mini-series Andersonville, as well as wrote, produced, and appeared in the History Channel documentary Vietnam Homecoming.

Vaughan's books have hit the NYT bestseller list seven times. He has won the Spur Award, the Porgie Award in Best Paperback Original, the Western Fictioneers Lifetime Achievement Award, the Readwest President's Award for Excellence in Western Fiction, and is a member of the American Writers Hall of Fame and a Pulitzer Prize nominee.

He is also a retired army officer, helicopter pilot with three tours in Vietnam, who has received the Distinguished Flying Cross, the Purple Heart, The Bronze Star with three oak leaf clusters, the Air Medal for valor with 35 oak leaf clusters, the Army Commendation Medal, the Meritorious Service Medal, and the Vietnamese Cross of Gallantry.

Made in United States
Troutdale, OR
03/10/2024

18357204R00116